Sathya Ramaganapathy is a humourist with two kids, the ulnar nerve and a long memory, especially for inconsequential things and old grievances. Armed with these, she conjures up what she believes are brilliantly funny and incisive pieces on parenting, kids and life in general.

She is the author of a parenting blog by the same name and her previously published children's books include *Cubby and His Rings*, *Cubby's Colours* and *Coo Taga Tak Tak*. Her work has appeared in several literary magazines and she was recently featured in the anthologies *Voices from the Attic* and *The Madras Mag*'s *Anthology of Contemporary Writing*.

She blogs at http://sathyarg.com

KICKASS PARENTING

Sathya Ramaganapathy

For Swaminathan,
I couldn't have done it without you. Any of it.

Published by
Rupa Publications India Pvt. Ltd 2018
7/16, Ansari Road, Daryaganj
New Delhi 110002

Sales centres:
Allahabad Bengaluru Chennai
Hyderabad Jaipur Kathmandu
Kolkata Mumbai

Copyright © Sathya Ramaganapathy 2018

This is a work of fiction. Names, characters, places and incidents are either the product of the author's imagination or are used fictitiously and any resemblance to any actual person, living or dead, events or locales is entirely coincidental.

All rights reserved.
No part of this publication may be reproduced, transmitted, or stored in a retrieval system, in any form or by any means, electronic, mechanical, photocopying, recording or otherwise, without the prior permission of the publisher.

ISBN: 978-81-291-5190-2

First impression 2018

10 9 8 7 6 5 4 3 2 1

The moral right of the author has been asserted.

Printed by HT Media Ltd, Gr. Noida

This book is sold subject to the condition that it shall not, by way of trade or otherwise, be lent, resold, hired out, or otherwise circulated, without the publisher's prior consent, in any form of binding or cover other than that in which it is published.

Contents

In the Beginning   vii

Summer Holidays: April–May
1. It's a Reader   3
2. All in a Day's Work   11
3. It's Not Fair   19
4. Exercising Your Voice—Pitch, Intensity and Modulation   27
5. Help for Hassled Homies   34

First Term: June–September
6. Math Is Fun. Not.   43
7. The Legion Extraordinaire   52
8. If It's Dinner, It Must Be Dosa   60
9. In Which We Talk about Something Embarrassing   66
10. Mind Your Language   72
11. Tongue-in-Cheek   76

Second Term: October–December
12. Pet Peeves   83
13. 'Aap Kaunse College Mein Ho?'   89
    (Which college do you study in?)

14. Let's Do the 'Haka'	96
15. Sartorially Speaking	101
16. Hold the Bus	110
17. We Don't Need No Education	116
18. What's in a Word?	124

Third Term: January–March

19. There's a Lizard in My Kitchen	133
20. Mission Accomplished	140
21. The Tooth Fairy Has Left the Building	143
22. Milestone Mammas	149
23. Is this the End?	155

In the Beginning

It is a truth universally acknowledged that a modern mom in possession of a cheeky kid must be in want of a singularly thick skin, or a doubly great sense of humour. Preferably, both.

I am blessed with not one, but two cheeky kids. Parenting is a veritable minefield in my household. Backchat and bad jokes, cheekiness and mischievous gleam in the eyes, pre-teen hormones and emotional meltdowns (of the parental variety). Every day is fraught with danger.

Take this morning for example. After reading about the Valentine's Day in the newspaper, my older daughter comes up to me and says, 'Amma, do you know it is romance day tomorrow?'

'Please call and ask Appa what he's planning to do about romancing me,' I instruct her. Pat comes the reply, 'Amma, umm...what are YOU planning to do about romancing Appa?'

I have determinedly resisted the urge to wring my hands and cry. Instead, I have stoically settled down to do what every self-respecting parent would do on finding herself in a similar situation. I have taken refuge in the final frontier—the Internet.

A tweet here, a blog there. I have begun chronicling this

all too familiar saga. The epic struggle between the parent and the smart alec child. It is a war out there, but I have realized I am not alone. There is a whole legion of beleaguered parents. Show me a parent who has never heard a 'Isn't it enough that I do my homework? Why do I have to "take an interest" in it?' and I will show you a unicorn.

My daughter tells me I should write a book.

'You keep talking about it all the time. You should write a big book.'

'Shall I quit my job and do it then?' I ask.

'Amma, I go to school for eight hours, I learn to play the keyboard, I read a lot, I go to sleep one hour before you…and I still manage to write every day!'

Just you wait kiddo, just you wait.

And thus was born *It's a Mom Thing*. This book is a tribute, dedicated to all those harassed moms and dads out there fighting the daily battles of parenthood. We shall prevail. This too shall pass.

Summer Holidays:
April–May

From: MyKidsSchool@Bengaluru.com
To: Amma@gmail.com
Date: Wednesday, 25 March 2015 at 10.48 AM

Subject: End of academic year 2014–2015

Dear Parent,

Greetings!

This is to inform you that the last working day for the school will be Friday, 27 March 2015. As always, we would like to insist that the children attend school till the last working day.
The new academic year will begin on Monday, 01 June 2015.
We wish you happy holidays and look forward to seeing the children in the next academic year.

With warm regards,
Principal

'Amma, you only said we could not bring a book to the dining table. You didn't say anything about us reading the cereal box or the jam bottle.'

1

It's a Reader

I am lying flat on my back in the operation theatre, OT as they call it, staring at the sharp lights overhead. I'm scared. You know, the stomach churning, finger wringing, wish-I-had-studied-more kind of feeling you get just before the exam. When you know you haven't prepared well enough and it's too late to do anything about it. That kind of scared. It is a theatre, after all. One has to be prepared for some drama.

'What's the matter?' asks the gynaecologist.

'Doctor I read every chapter of *What to Expect When You're Expecting*. Except the one on C-sections. I can't believe that the one topic I did not study is the only one I am being tested on.'

The doctor looks over at the anaesthetist and the paediatrician, and they barely manage to hold their laughter.

At least somebody is having a good time, I think, disgruntled.

I won't go into the gory details of what happens next. In typical filmi style, I hear a cry and the doctor grandly announces—'It's a reader!'

They bring her over to me and I peer at her. I seem to be looking at everything through a haze, my contact lenses being out. I can't quite make out what she looks like. But this I do see. She holds her hands up, palms folded inwards, almost as if she were holding a book in front of her. And I remember being so pleased. A reader! I had always wanted one.

A few years later, the same place, the same people. The doctor even slides in a joke about me being better prepared for the exam this time around, and then she announces—'It's another reader!' And, just like that, our family unit is complete.

∽

As you might have guessed by now, we are a family that reads. There are books, books everywhere…as far as the eyes can see, which is not that far, considering we live in an apartment. As with every modern apartment, we are short of space. Stacked on the floor next to the sofa in the living room, piled high under the bed, on the bedside tables, in the loft, stacked randomly on every open surface available. I am known to occasionally lose my temper over the mess and threaten to give it all away. Even as our cheap particle board bookshelves teeter under the weight of the books, we are stubbornly resisting the call of the Kindle. We might just move to real wood.

From the youngest kid to the oldest grandfather, everybody in our family reads. The little one, all of nine, has a quirky sense of humour. A giggle here, a chortle there, a loud guffaw... it's as if her funny bone is waiting to be tickled. She likes to, nay, she insists on reading out aloud every funny passage in full detail and with great animation. 'You get it?' she asks in excitement, even as she trips over the words in the hurry to get to the punchline. God forbid if you don't laugh. 'Tsk, tsk, whatever happened to your sense of humour?' A sad shake of her head. 'Wait Amma, I'll read it out to you again.' And you better listen to the whole passage all over again.

The older one, eleven years old, reads like there is no tomorrow. In the absence of a book, she will even read the labels on cereal boxes and jam bottles. She can be found hanging off the armrest of the sofa—the book resting on the ground, lying upside down on the seat, feet up on the back of the sofa—book in hand, slouched on the bed—book propped up on her crossed leg, standing up, walking, in fact she is known to read in all positions, except sitting upright.

She is, like all pre-teens, currently fascinated by fantasy fiction. And to my surprise, the newspaper. As I pick her up from the bus stop in the evening, she asks, 'What's the news today, Amma?'

One of the first things she does when she comes home is to look for the newspaper.

'Amma where is the sports page?' she asks, annoyed to find the papers not in order and some pages missing.

'Have you looked for it in its usual place?' I ask her.

'You mean the magazine holder?'

'No, the bathroom.'

She has now taken to reprimanding her father on her way out of the door in the morning. 'Appa, please leave the paper in order!'

The husband is a staunch follower of all things determinedly non-fiction (read: boring). Large, heavy tomes expounding upon India-before-Independence, India-after-Independence, Gandhi-before India-before Independence, Gandhi-after India-after Independence—you get the drift. He claims he likes to read before he goes to sleep. I suspect he *needs* them to fall asleep.

The grandfather is the sole reader of all books populist, leftist, Tamil, and magazines whose continuing publication is probably down to his lone surviving subscription.

Then there is me. Depending on what strikes my fancy at the moment, I read whodunnits, literary fiction, classics, thrillers and short stories. Under duress, I will admit to being a sucker for historical romance. The one thing I do not read is non-fiction. Seeing the husband snoring away under one of those is enough. What I love above all is children's fiction. As you can imagine, with two kids, I got to read a lot of that. Of course, it can get to you, when you are asked to read a book again and again and yet again for the…let's see…three thousand and sixteenth time. Back in the day, if you woke me up in the middle of the night, I could've recited *The Cat in the Hat* or *The Gruffalo*, eyes closed.

I remember friends and family laughing at me when I began reading to my kids when they were young. 'They won't understand anything, it's too early.' Oh alright, I admit, they were only three months old. But I was on a mission. I wanted to introduce them to the joy of books, the best that the written word had to offer. And I wanted to get an early start.

My kids were, of course, enthralled. Or maybe they were just thinking, *It's showtime! Let's see what this silly Amma is going to get up to today.* As I enthusiastically enacted scenes with gusto, putting on different voices for different characters, maybe they were thinking, *Why is she making those faces? Poor thing, she is trying so hard. Let's clap.* Maybe they were just amused by what a fool I was making of myself.

All that is water under the bridge now.

We read a lot in those early years. From the genius simplicity of Eric Carle, to the madness of Dr Seuss, to the magic of Julia Donaldson. We marched our way through the prolific Enid Blyton, the deliciously wicked Roald Dahl and the endless Amar Chitra Kathas, until we reached a turning point with J.K. Rowling and Rick Riordan. A coming of age, so to say, as the kids began to devour books on their own—Ruskin Bond, Satyajit Ray, P.G. Wodehouse and newer writers of dark fantasy fiction I knew nothing about. I do not read to the kids anymore, they are too old for that.

As they grow older, the kids no longer look to me alone for book recommendations. However, what's worse is that they now challenge my authority over the bookshelf itself. Any true book lover would know that there is only one sensible way to organize a bookshelf. First by genre (say whodunnits); author in genre (strictly in alphabetical order); if the author has a series, arrange it in chronological order; in the absence of a series, arrange by the book height. The kids however, want to experiment. Colour coding this week, ordered by height the next, most favourite to least favourite…whatever will they come up with next.

In this epic territorial struggle, I finally agree, albeit reluctantly, to let them do their thing with the children's books if they let the adult books be. It's surely a passing phase. Kids get distracted. In no time at all the books will go back to being arranged the right way. My way.

Considering the lack of space in most modern apartments, it is inevitable that we have to carefully pick what we buy. The rest we borrow. The first thing I look for in any locality I move into is the library. And a good tailor, of course. That comes a close second. The kids and I share a library membership.

When our favourite library around the corner, 'Easy Library', shut shop recently, unable to survive in this tussle between non-readers and e-book readers, our collective hearts broke. What would we do? Without those books hidden away in some nook of the library, brittle pages, yellowing and spotted with age, smelling that old book smell. Without the friendly owner to chat with us and recommend delightful new reads. Without our librarian to keep aside our favourite authors and quietly waive off the twelve-books-per-visit rule simply because, really, how on earth could we make do with just twelve books? What would we do?

Left with no other option, we move to another library. A chain this time. This one is even closer, just a few minutes' walk from our home. Spacious, air-conditioned, better organized. Their books are shiny and new, their catalogue is online and you can even order across all branches. It's all computerized and self-service.

'What is the biggest membership plan you have?' I ask the lady at the desk.

'Four books per visit,' she says.

I stare in shock. Four books. Three readers. How will we cope?

'But you can come every day and exchange the books, if

you want,' she says.

How can I explain to this impersonal shop attendant, for she is certainly no librarian, the joy of having books stacked on the bedside table, letting your mood dictate what you want to read?

But it seems my daughters and I have no choice. The summer holidays are upon us and we cannot survive the two months in close quarters without books to keep us sane. So we settle for the four-book plan and come to an agreement about how we will share the books. During the school holidays the kids will split the four books whichever way they wish between themselves and during the school year, I will get two books, and the kids, one each.

∽

I must confess that I often complain that my kids read too much. My friends tell me this is a good problem to have. But I worry that they will be so lost in these imaginary worlds of theirs that they will miss out on living in this very real one.

In my family we were not allowed to read at the dining table as kids. 'It is disrespectful to the food and the person who put in so much effort to make it,' my mother used to say. So in sheer perversity, I let my kids read at the table. But when there are days I have slaved over some dish, only to see them blindly eat it without tasting it, or when I ask how dinner was, to hear them mumble casually 'Yeah, it was ok,' I fume. And I think of my mother. And I rescind the rule.

But more often than not, I let them read whenever and wherever they want. I guess it all depends on how much or how little I want to engage with them at a given time. Devious, I know. And it is probably confusing to the kids that I chide them for reading some of the times and not others. What the heck, I am the adult here. I don't have to explain everything, do I?

The one good thing with all this reading business is that when it comes to birthdays, the presents are easy to figure out. No agonizing over which game or toy or accessory to get. The kids are happy to present us with a list beforehand and we are happy to buy it for them, throwing in an additional new author or two as a surprise.

My older daughter's twelfth birthday is coming up soon and with it, the promise of the big 'teens' just round the corner.

'What do you want for your birthday?' I ask her, expecting the usual list of books.

'Can you get me a Kindle?' she asks hopefully.

Et tu, Brute?

Her: Appa, who is a CEO?
Appa: A Chief Executive Officer is the head of a company.
Her: So does a CEO execute the officers who don't do their work properly?

2

All in a Day's Work

As a kid, one of the things I used to look forward to was the beginning of a new month. Every new month would bring with it a new edition of the *Reader's Digest*. Everybody in my family kept an eye on the postbox, hoping to catch the magazine first. I would try to negotiate with my parents, promising not to take more than ten minutes. All I wanted to read were the humour columns. 'Life's Like That', 'Humour in Uniform', 'All in a Day's Work'. What fun these workplaces must be, I remember thinking. There was always something interesting happening. I wanted to go to one too, when I grew up.

I did, of course. Grow up and go to an office. But to my immense disappointment, the humorous moments were few and far in between. Work was far more mundane than I had imagined it to be.

My daughters are curious too. About work and workplaces. 'What do you do at work?' is an oft-repeated question in my family. Especially when they are at home during the holidays. Like now. They have a lot of time on their hands and they get to see what our day typically looks like when they are away at school. This question about what we do at work is usually directed at their father. I often work from home, a flexibility and luxury that the start-up I work with affords me. So my daughters are not quite as curious about my work. They see me settle down in the morning at my desk with my laptop. Sometimes they come and look over my shoulder as I work on a presentation. They know all about PowerPoint and Skype. They see me get on calls with my colleagues and clients, putting on my 'work voice'. They know enough not to come into my room when I am on a call. There is no mystery there.

But that is not the case with their father who works long hours outside the home. One of the decisions we took early on as parents was to set predictable bedtime routine for the kids. This meant, among other things, going to bed early. It meant that during the weekdays the kids would not see their father at night since his timings were unpredictable and he would often return home way past their bedtime. In fact, when he left for work in the mornings, the kids would laughingly call out to him, 'Bye Appa, see you tomorrow'. Is it any wonder then that they are curious about his workplace?

A few years ago when my older daughter turned five, we asked her if she wanted to do something special on her birthday.

'I want to go to Appa's office,' she said.

Of all the things she could've asked, the only thing she really wanted to do was to see this enchanted, magical place her father disappeared off to every morning.

So he took her to his office for a couple of hours that day. She got duly pampered by his colleagues. Who can resist a cute and adorable five-year-old? Obviously the husband didn't get any work done that morning and she didn't really get to see anything of the work that goes on in an office or what he actually did every day at work.

My younger daughter is just as intrigued by her father's work and workplace. She has often heard about this special treat her older sister got on her birthday and wants one too. 'Appa, it is summer holidays now. I don't have school. So can I come with you to your office?' she pesters him. 'Hmm...not today. It's going to be a busy day today,' he says.

'What do you do at the office, Appa?' she asks.

'Well, there are a lot of people in my office. I manage them, give them work and tell them what to do,' answers the husband simply, in an attempt to unravel the vast underbelly that is 'management' in the corporate world.

'Oh, so they do all the work in your office. Then, besides giving work to other people, what do YOU actually do?'

∽

Have you ever thought about how hard it is to explain just exactly what it is we do at work? Especially to kids. I imagine some professions are easier to explain than others. Doctor, teacher, bus driver, fireman, policeman, architect, fashion designer. But how does one explain application services or investment banking to a nine-year-old?

'I don't *get* banks,' says my younger daughter. I remember, when I was a kid, my father would sometimes take me along with him when he went to the bank. When I was six years old, he took me to meet the bank manager, a friendly gentleman who gave me a piggy bank. Only, it was not a pig, but a lion. It was made of shiny plastic, the head of the lion painted in sunny yellow, with a cylindrical base in gun-metal blue. He told me that I should use it to save money at home. And then when I had enough saved up, he said that I should visit the bank again to deposit my money there so it would grow 'bigger' and 'bigger'. I remember being thrilled at the prospect of my own money.

But in this age of mobile, Internet banking and 'relationship managers', how is one to show a kid what a bank is or to experience the thrill of learning about multiplying your money from a genial bank manager? At most, you can take a kid to the ATM.

Today, I have decided to take my younger daughter along when I go to the ATM.

'So if you want money, do you just go to an ATM? Will it give the money to anyone?' she asks, her eyes wide with wonder.

I explain to her about having an account with the bank, depositing money and then withdrawing it when one needs. I even give her a mini lesson on the cost of servicing a walk-in customer at the bank and the convenience of an ATM.

'Oh, I always thought that the machine was just a front,' she says innocently. 'I thought there's a room behind the machine where a lot of people sit in rows with piles of money in front of them. So when we punch in the amount we want, a screen shows them that number. Then, they count the money and put it into the back of the machine and it then spits out the money to us.'

I don't think I am quite ready to explain investment banking to her.

∽

I have had a relatively easier time explaining my job to the kids. Especially when compared to the husband who works, as it happens, in applications services.

'I work in marketing, specifically digital marketing,' I tell the girls when they ask me what my job is.

'Does that mean you sell your company's product to customers?'

I hesitate, deliberating whether I should explain the difference between sales and marketing.

'Marketing is making people want to buy something.'

'How do you do that?'

'We do lots of different things to make people know about our product. For example, suppose our company were to sell cookies, we would make advertisements about these cookies. Then, you would see these ads on TV, radio, newspaper and on the Internet. So the next time you are in a shop looking to buy cookies, you would immediately think of our company. Sometimes you might not even be thinking of buying cookies, but when you are in the supermarket and you see our cookie on a shelf, you might remember our ad and decide to try it.'

They get it immediately. I am rather proud of having condensed Philip Kotler's voluminous Marketing Management and the four P's quite succinctly. But of course that is not the end of the matter. A few days later while they were watching a cricket match on TV, they kept seeing a certain cookie advertisement, playing over and over again. Alas, with the veil now lifted off their eyes, this is what my older daughter had to say, 'I don't know why companies advertise so aggressively. It's not like we pay attention or anything. And it's not like we are going to buy something just because we saw an ad on TV or Subway Surfer.'

I don't know whether the mother in me should feel happy at not being pestered anymore with unnecessary purchases or the marketer in me should bemoan the loss of a future customer.

∫

When she was two, my older daughter wanted to be a gardener. There's water. There's mud. Deliciously squishy mush that you can sink your hands into. What's not to like? When she was six, she wanted to be an 'acrobatic, inventor scientist who also cooks'. Now at age eleven, she thinks that while the coolest job in the world is that of a librarian, she wants to be an 'engineer, author, architect and lawyer'.

The one job whose demands she understands very well, I think, is that of being a mom. Recently, on a weekend getaway with my parents, she kept asking me questions, pestering me to do something or the other with her.

'I'm off duty today. Ask *thatha* (grandfather), he is in charge,' I told her.

'Amma, a mother is always on duty!' she said. And that was that.

The advantage of my working from home is that my kids

actually see me work, especially like now, when they are at home during the holidays.

'Amma, you work so hard!' exclaimed my older daughter to me at the end of one particularly hectic workday. There had been a flurry of calls all day, and I was frantically coordinating with different team members to send something out before a five o'clock deadline. Right after that, I had to drive her to her music class, and once we came home it was time to prepare dinner for the family. I must confess, I was secretly thrilled that she had noticed and, yes I admit, that she admired me for doing it all. Who wouldn't?

The flip side of this is that the kids are not always too sure about their father. And they often tease him about it. You can see how this might work out in my favour though.

'What is this, Appa? Amma takes care of us, she does everything around the house and she has to do office work too.'

'Ah, but I put the bread on the table!' says the husband loftily.

'Appa...' they groan, dissolving in a fit of giggles. They do love a good pun. And it *is* the husband's job to stop by at the popular Thom's bakery on his way home from work to buy our daily bread.

It is only recently that they have conceded that even though they have not seen enough evidence, their father might just be working very hard as well. So when they call him at work, the first thing they now ask is 'Are you busy? Are you in a meeting?'

∽

Today, the husband has come home a little early. He has some news. My younger daughter who inevitably has one ear tuned in to all our conversations, becomes curious when she overhears the words 'new job'.

'What are you talking about, Appa?' she asks.

'I have a new job,' he says.

'Oh, are you joining a new company?' she asks.

'No, I am still with the same company. I just have a new role.'

'Oh,' she says mulling this over. 'But are you still ordering people about in your office or do you actually have to work?'

> Older daughter: Stop irritating me.
> Younger daughter: I am not irritating you.
> *You* are getting irritated.

3

It's Not Fair

Whistle. Hold the thumb and the index finger together in an 'A-Okay' sign. Place it under the tip of the tongue. Then push to roll the tongue up so the tip almost touches the top of the mouth. Almost, but not quite. Then blow. Hard. A shrill, piercing whistle, guaranteed to break up even the most determined sibling bickering.

If there is one thing I wish I knew how to do, it would be to whistle. I've tried my hand at it. Whistling with just your lips doesn't quite seem to have the same impact. So I've tried all the finger variations: one hand—two fingers; two hands—two fingers; two hands—four fingers. I have had very little success. I am told by those in the know, that with enough practice, I should be able to get the hang of it. In a year or four.

I am quite disappointed they don't make this a mandatory skill for all parents-to-be. Like those blood tests and ultrasounds. They should insist on a whistle test. Especially for second-time parents. Getting the baby to burp? Anybody can do that. Potty training? Come on. But whistle? That's a tough one to learn. And indispensable for a parent dealing with siblings. Especially during holidays.

School holidays. Arggh. I hate summer holidays. To be fair, I hate Dussehra holidays and winter holidays as well. I hate any kind of school holiday. Period. Obviously, I loved them all as a kid. Couldn't wait for them to come around soon enough. But I hate them as a parent. What could be less fun than having two perpetually bored, hungry, and, lest we forget, squabbling kids cooped up in the house for days together?

Among the various roles I juggle in my life, the hardest one is that of a referee. It's not unlike a professional sport. Games run afoul. There's sledging, heckling, tackling, kicking. In most sports though, you have a second referee to assist the main one. In cricket, you even have third umpires who have access to video replays. But in reality, when you are called in to referee an argument or a fight between your kids, more often than not, your spouse is not around to consult with. As expected, they conveniently disappear at just the right moment, only to reappear once everything is sorted out. So it's your call, and yours alone to make. There will be appeals, impassioned ones at that. Two wildly different versions of the same story. And tears galore. No matter how hard you try to be fair, you will end up having to take sides. You can never win.

Ah, the joys of sibling rivalry.

My older daughter says, 'Everything is always my fault. Just because I am older, you expect me to be more understanding and give in. She does whatever she wants and gets away with it by crying. You lecture only me. You never tell her anything. Why can't you tell her to be less annoying?'

My younger daughter says, 'Just because she is older, she gets to be the first in everything. Why should she be the only one to decide what we should play or what treat we should get? Why can't I pick? She gets to do all the interesting stuff. Why can't I stay up late? Why can't I read this book or go for a sleepover?'

I am no expert and I wouldn't want to generalize, but it seems to me that there is a pattern to the kids' behaviour, one that repeats itself over and over again. What is it with older siblings and bossiness? And younger siblings and peskiness? The smug know-it-all and the annoying mock-it-all. I'm sure there is a middle child syndrome and an only child syndrome as well. Only, I am not familiar with them.

In my house, it all begins quite innocuously. After some discussion, they settle down to play a game of Monopoly. Usually there is some friendly verbal banter. Before you blink, it turns into a full-blown argument.

'Amma, she is not following the rules,' says my older daughter in a superior tone.

'Yeah right! Amma, she is making up the rules just like that,' retorts the feisty younger one.

'Amma, tell her to listen to me. And tell her to stop making faces at me.' Mockery is my younger daughter's weapon of choice, and over the years, she has honed it to perfection.

'Amma, she hit me...'

'Amma...'

When it moves to hand-to-hand combat, you know it's time to intervene. Friends with older kids tell me that I need to take a step back. 'Let them resolve their own fights. Don't jump in all the time.' Their theory is that, left to their own devices, the kids will find a way to resolve their issues. They will figure it out. Only, my kids don't seem to have heard this theory. They insist that I get involved and resolve every dispute. They don't let me get away so easily. If I don't learn to whistle soon, at the very least I need to figure out how to pull the Houdini act.

∽

If you think holidays are tough, schooldays are no less challenging. Every morning I wake up and I pray for a non-combat day. Some days I am lucky.

'Can I go for a bath first today?' asks the older one.

'Ok,' says the younger one.

Bullet dodged.

Some days I am not.

'I want to go for a bath first today,' demands the older one.

'But you got to go first yesterday,' retorts the younger one.

'So what? Last week you got to go first two days in a row.'

Their memory for such details is impeccable.

'It's my turn to go first today,' insists the younger one.

'But Amma, she takes so much time. Whenever she goes first, she makes me late for school,' wails the older one.

I decide that the only way to resolve this issue is to go about it in a logical and systematic manner. I mark out alternate days in the calendar so each one will get a turn at having their bath first. The husband scoffs. We pay him no heed. We rarely do.

There are a few trade-ins here and there. But sooner or later, we lose track of whose turn it is that day and we are back to square one.

And so it goes, most mornings, bickering back and forth, till we deposit the kids in the school bus. I do not know what happens after that and I do not want to know either. It's not in my job description.

The evenings are no better. They have had a long day at school. They are tired, hungry and cranky. Itching to pick a fight. It's almost as if they cannot help themselves.

'Amma, she took the book I was reading,' complains the older one.

'But you put the book down,' says the younger.

'Yeah, to go to the bathroom.'

'How was I to know that?'

'Now I've lost my page,' whines the older one.

'As if I care,' sneers the younger one, making a face at her older sister.

'Amma, she is mocking me.'

'No mocking,' I call out.

'You always pick on me,' says the younger one and it all ends in tears.

∽

They watch me like hawks, these kids of mine. Waiting to catch me out. To see if I am favouring one over the other. And they have a phenomenal memory. They remember every rule, every decision, every slight, every infraction. How come you let her read *Harry Potter* now, whereas I was allowed to read it only after

I turned ten? How come she gets to stay up late and I don't?

I tell them over and over again that the rules are the same, but they are different people and the situations are different each time. I have to treat each case individually.

A while ago, at the end of last year's school term, the kids fell sick, one after the other. While one stayed home, the other went to school. Needless to say, they compared notes at the end of the day and this is what I got to hear:

'Amma, you gave her soup and toast? When I was unwell, you only gave me idli and curd. It's just not fair.'

I tried to explain.

'She has a sore throat and soup is soothing for that. But you had an upset stomach. Idli is light on the stomach and you know that curd has all the good bacteria. So I made them especially for you.'

'Still. It's not fair.'

It never is. Yet another case in point is grapes.

My kids love grapes and come winter, we have the choicest pickings—the Bangalore Blues, Thomson Seedless, Flame, Sharad, Red Globe, Sonika. The problem though is division. Irrespective of how careful I am about giving them similar portions, they compare each other's bowls and find theirs falling short. I tell them that in the long run it all evens out. But to no avail. On principle I refuse to count the grapes. Else next they'll have me counting the pomegranate seeds. I refuse to buy a weighing scale too. Instead I decide to pass the grape back to their court, so to say. I wash the grapes. Then I ask one of them to distribute it equally. Approximating it, no counting allowed. Once that is done, the other person gets to pick the bowl of their choice. Distribution and selection, two contentious issues thus settled. Game, set and match, if I may say so myself. I suspect they are still unhappy, and they still find their portions falling short, but they can no longer fault me. At least, not on this.

∽

All's not lost though. It's not doom and gloom all the time. There are moments, not all that uncommon, especially as they grow older, when they agree to be agreeable. Small pockets of calm when the two settle upon a common activity or a game and proceed to engage with each other. However, I must warn you, if you haven't heard a peep from them for more than a couple of hours, they must be up to something. Time to step in.

I complain sometimes about all the refereeing I have to do every day. So I am often at the receiving end of well-meaning advice from friends and family. About how my kids are angels, and how well-behaved they are when the husband and I are not around. How I should react swiftly, as soon as I see the signs of a fight brewing, and distract them. This the last thing I want to hear. I don't like conversations that don't go my way.

The best conversations are the ones where I can grumble, only to have a friend pick up the ball and lob it right back at me, with a story of her own. About the battle for the bunk bed and the unfair division of the mangoes. About verbal spats and physical scraps. About how tough it is to mediate. The unfairness of it all. We can shake our heads together, sigh and feel better already.

The husband though has a different opinion. He refuses to take all this very seriously. If I ever grumble about the constant mediation and peacekeeping, he only has this to say, 'But you would be so bored without all this excitement.'

Sometimes I wonder what life would be like in a single child family. Quieter, probably. Then I wonder what life would be like in a family with three or four children, the kids outnumbering the parents. And I think to myself, this is good. Until I hear them call out:

'Amma, she pinched me.'

'No, she elbowed me first.'

'But she was making faces at me.'

Dear God, please give me the patience to handle this. And a whistle.

> 'I don't know how you have this effect, Amma. Whenever you say 'do what you want, it's your choice' in THAT voice, I just feel compelled to do what YOU want me to do. You should teach me that voice.'

4

Exercising Your Voice—Pitch, Intensity and Modulation

'Girls... time to wake up *kanna* (darling),' I call out as I walk in to my daughters' room one morning. My older daughter tells me, 'Amma, do you know you wake us up with the exact same words in the exact same tone every single morning.' Let's not forget, the exact same time as well. Call me a creature of habit. But she's right.

Why do we say the same things over and over again? Comb your hair. Wash your hands. Wash your feet. Hang out the towel. Put away your bag. Do your homework. Put the shoes in the closet. Practise your keyboard lesson. Comb your hair. Did I already say that? Well, comb it again. It looks like a bird's nest.

I must confess to having a vague memory of my mother repeatedly asking me to comb my hair (ok, maybe it's not so vague). But you wouldn't know when you look at me now. A perfect blunt cut, every hair in place. Always. Is it because of my mother that I am obsessed...err, have well-groomed hair? Or, is it in spite of her? Either ways, it's easier to blame it on the parents.

Hairy tales aside, why do we repeat ourselves? Yes, we know it all, we've seen it all, done it all, and we want to pass on all those pearls of wisdom to the torchbearers of the future. Of course, if you knew your gemology, you would know that pearls are nothing but disgusting secretions made by thick-shelled molluscs to cover up irritants that they cannot get rid of. That's right, when an irritant lodges itself in an oyster's body, then in order to protect itself, the oyster takes defensive action. It starts secreting a substance to cover the irritant, layer upon layer, all of which over time turns into a lustrous pearl. So much for pearls of wisdom.

Will repeating ourselves again, and again, and yet again, for the umpteenth time, just in case they missed it, actually impress upon the kids any better? Will our words gradually worm their way into the kids' inner consciousness, only to magically reappear at just the right moment so we can proudly pat ourselves on our backs and say, 'Well done you!' Or maybe, just maybe, they will get fed up with us going on and on, and simply give in and do it? Yeah, right.

Are we fooling ourselves? Are we just background noise?

Kids have selective hearing at best. 'Sometimes we like to shut off our ears. It depends on what we want to hear' says my daughter who can hear me gossiping with her dad in the next room, but turns a deaf ear when asked to clean the table. This is why it is of utmost importance that we master *The Voice*. It's not enough to just say something. We need to say it the right way. A slight change in the tone, sometimes the pitch, maybe it's in the intonation, a lilt or the cadence, perhaps it's the undertone, or just plain volume. Subtle nuances that make all the difference. A voice for everything and everything in its voice.

This is especially important during the holidays, when the kids are around all day, getting on each other's and your nerves all the time. It can seem overwhelming at first. To get the voice right. To know what and how to say or not say something. So let me lay it all out for you.

The urgent, low-pitched, furious, you-better-listen-to-me-now-or-else-there-will-be-murder voice: This one is reserved for public spaces. Imagine this. You are at the supermarket. After an hour of traipsing through the aisles, you reach the checkout counter and that's when your kids spot the stash of candy. Rows upon rows of shiny bars, Cadbury's Silk, Kit Kats, and Perks, and the mints and the dreaded chewing gums, stacked right next to the checkout counter with the express intention of tempting your children.

The kids have seen it and they want it. Now. You say no, of course. You try reasoning, you try pleading. All the while the folks in the queue behind you, the women at the counter, the security guards at the door, the floor supervisor—all strangers—are looking at you. You, the Chocolate Nazi! Now the important thing to remember here is that the kids know exactly what they are doing. They know you'll say no to the chocolate, but they also know that this is perhaps their best chance and place to put you in a spot. So, you bend down, lower your voice to a harsh whisper and then let it rip: 'If you do not put down that Kit Kat right this minute, you can forget about getting that Pokémon monster collection (or Lego bricks or the Frozen Elsa doll) for your birthday and I will throw out the rest of your card/bricks/doll collection too.' You give a tight smile for all the world to see—see, there's nothing wrong—even as you mutter dire consequences under your breath. More often than not, the kids will cave in. Unless, of course, if you are dealing with a toddler, in which case, all I can say is good luck.

The oh-I-am-so-calm-because-I-want-you-to-think-I-am-cool voice: The key here is that I want you to *think* I am cool. But I am oh-so-not-cool with this. I'm sure you've been there. Situations where you're being put in a spot in front of friends and acquaintances. You are at a birthday party. As you get ready to leave, the host whips out the return gift. Now if you know anything at all about birthday parties, you would know that the most important part of the party is the return gift or the party favours. Kids act like they have ants in their pants till they get them. Or maybe that's just down to all that soda. Hosts spend sleepless nights trying to come up with interesting return gifts.

This time it's a—drum roll please—fish. A fish! All those years your kids have begged, whined, thrown tantrums for a pet and now it's just been handed to them on a platter…err…a plastic bag (a fish on a platter would be too gross). The kids look at you. Waiting, watching. They know your views on pets. More on that later.

Inside, you are seething. But you put on a light airy voice. 'Oh it's a fish. That's so nice,' you coo.

'It's a Betta fish, they're fighter fish,' your host tells you helpfully.

You manage a weak smile. You do want to keep up appearances.

The kids can't believe their luck. 'Can we keep it? Can we keep it?' They jump up and down in excitement. You give them the stare. But you have lost the battle and they know it. Damn, what's wrong with giving a potted plant?

The firm voice: This one is important to learn. Kids need to know that there are boundaries. There will be times when you have to lay down the law. Do it in no uncertain terms. If you blink, or show any signs of wavering, they will latch on to that hesitancy. 'Wash your hands before dinner', 'Go to bed at eight'. Kids will know this is the line and they will toe it. You might hear a minor grumble or two, but not to worry, that's all on par.

The garden variety do-it-now bark: This one is straightforward. And it works. You just raise your voice and tell them in no uncertain terms what you want them to do. The kids call it shouting. 'Amma, instead of shouting at me, if you said it to me in a normal voice, I would listen,' says my daughter. As if.

Let me tell you about this experiment I did recently. Mean of me to experiment on the kids, I know, but it's all for a greater common good. The girls had been complaining that I was raising my voice all the time. So when I recently caught them playing on the iPad for hours on end, I rolled up my sleeves and this is what happened.

'Can you stop playing on the iPad?' That's me in a calm, measured voice no one could take offence at. No response.

Not even a blink.

'Can you please stop playing on the iPad?' Me again, still in that same calm voice, and I even added a please. Still no response.

'CAN YOU STOP PLAYING ON THE iPAD?' I hollered.

Sure enough, they surfaced from their Minecraft-induced daze only to say, 'You didn't have to shout Amma. You could've told us nicely.'

You get the picture? Now that you get where I am going with this, here are a few more voices you could sink your teeth into.

The sarcastic, 'yeah right' voice: I wouldn't recommend this one at all. It does nothing for anyone. Sure, you might get a momentary rush of relief delivering that snarky, biting set-down, but believe me, it vanishes faster than you can say *gajar ka halwa* and all you are left with is a deep, abiding sense of disgust at yourself for sinking so low. As for the kids, the last thing you want to do is scar them for life. Well, not deliberately.

The honeyed, butter-wouldn't-melt-in-your-mouth voice: Personally, this one would score an 'F' in my house. My kids would see through it in a jiffy. Maybe it's me. And before you judge me or make snarky comments, I do have a nice voice and I can be sweet. Kind of. Maybe it's my kids. They are instantly suspicious of anything that sounds like it is too good to be true. I find that straight talking works way better with them.

The martyred, oh-I-gave-up-so-much-for-you voice: We've all heard this one at one time or another in our lives. Lay on the guilt to get them to do what you want. Sure, it's blackmail, of the emotional variety. You've got to do what you've got to do. But my friends, with older kids especially, tell me that this voice loses its power very quickly. So use it judiciously.

The do-what-you-want-it's-your-choice voice: When delivered at just the right pitch, with the exact inflection, this is guaranteed to make the kids realize they can do anything but that. Nothing is explicitly stated, but there is an implied threat in the undertone. The direct threats, kids learn to handle that over time. But the unknown, that's a whole different ball game. This voice is tough to master, but once you get it, it's the most thrilling one of all.

The I-told-you-so voice: Isn't it wonderful to be proved right? The downside though is that it inevitably comes at the expense of the kids getting hurt, emotionally or physically. Didn't I tell you not to touch the kitchen knife? Didn't I tell you to pack your bag last night so you wouldn't forget the homework? While I love being right, I also hate it when I'm right. Go figure.

And then there are the silences. You can say so much without saying anything at all. Disappointment. Anger. Hurt. Rejection. Sadness. Fear. A friend once told me she feared silence the most. She grew up in a family where everything was no holds barred. Everybody was opinionated and not afraid to express it. There were always loud voices, raised in argument, excitement, anger, happiness. It was all out there. The silent treatment, she said, is one of the worst things you can mete out to a child.

I've personally tried them all. And I can tell you that they have all worked, at one time or another, with varying degrees of success. Except the hair. That still looks like a bird's nest.

> 'You can force me to help Amma hang out the clothes,
> but you can't force me to do it cheerfully!'

5

Help for Hassled Homies

'Amma, are you in a good mood now?' asks my younger daughter one lazy Sunday morning.

'Why?' I ask her.

'I want to ask you something. But I don't want to ask when you are in a bad mood.' Nine years old and she has already figured out how to play her cards.

I am suspicious and I am not sure where this is leading.

'Tell me,' I say reluctantly. It is the last thing I want to say and I know I will regret getting into this conversation.

'What do you think about me earning some money?'

Now this is completely out of the blue.

'Why? Why do you need money?'

'Amma, I just like the idea of earning my own money. And I will use the money to buy gifts for people, so I don't have to piggyback on your and Appa's gifts'.

Ah, now I see where this is coming from. Her older sister has recently given her a birthday present, separate from the gift we all gave together as a family. It was a set of pens that she had paid for herself, with some money she earned specifically for this purpose by doing a few chores around the house.

'Don't we always take your opinion before we buy a gift for anyone?' I ask, trying to deflect.

'Yes. But it's still not the same as giving my own gift.'

'Hmm.'

'So can I earn some money? Will you pay me if I do some chores around the house?'

I don't give her an answer. Yet.

She goes into her room and very shortly comes out with a handwritten flyer. It reads as follows:

Running out of time?
Simply not enthusiastic?
Then you need my services.
I'll do all your little tasks.

The list of tasks includes doing the dishes, washing windows, cleaning and organizing the bookshelves, going to the local store for small purchases and a few more. Each one can be commissioned for the princely sum of ₹1. The innocent babe.

'So...?' she asks eagerly.

'We'll see...' I say.

'Amma, you keep saying "we'll see" whenever we ask anything,' states my older daughter, jumping in to support her sister. 'By "we'll see" you obviously mean "no", but you just don't want to say it!' she says challengingly.

'I said I'll think about it and I will. If you pester me anymore, then the answer will really be a "NO",' I threaten.

∫

Later in the day, I put my feet up for a nap. Just as I drift off into a slumber, I'm woken up by whispering at the far end of the bedroom.

'Is she awake?' asks the younger one.

'No, I think she is asleep,' says the older one.

'Amma, are you awake?' asks the younger one in a faux whisper, as they both tiptoe closer.

I open my eyes and glare at them. Seeing my eyes open, they jump on to the bed excitedly.

'See Amma, we made a poster.'

It seems they have decided to team up and the poster is an advertisement for their services.

Help for Hassled Homies Agency

That is what they have decided to call themselves.

'Homies?' I ask them.

'Yes. Homies is our short-form for people who live in homes,' they assure me.

There are a lot of new items on the list now, including cleaning the refrigerator and other electronic items, caring for plants, making beds, room and wardrobe cleaning. They even offer special services such as entertainment should we feel bored, and moneylending. Yes, once they earn and save up enough, they tell me, they will be happy to lend us money should we ever fall short.

The poster also includes a revised rate card. The fees have

increased tenfold. It now ranges between ₹10 to ₹20 for services rendered. The kid has become wiser, courtesy older sister.

I am not quite sure what I should do. There are different schools of thought on this issue. When should you start giving kids pocket money? Should you give them pocket money at all? Is it correct to pay them for helping around the house? How much should you pay? How often? Weekly, monthly, pay-as-you-go? What about pay for performance? Two chores per day, three chores per day? How much is too much? A lot of questions, a lot of debate, but no clear conclusions.

After mulling over it for a while, I decide it is not such a bad idea after all. They are old enough to earn and manage their money, within reason. I like the idea of them taking on responsibilities. Experiencing the sense of satisfaction that comes with a job well done. Learning the value of money. Seeing what goes into the running of a house. Obviously, they will be thrilled to wash windows, clean the car. It will be like Tom Sawyer all over again. There's water, it is fun, what more could one ask for.

But there is also the sheer monotony of clothes to be washed, hung out to dry, folded, put back into the wardrobe. Only to be repeated all over again the next day. These are the daily routines that keep the home running like a well-oiled machine. You don't have to like it. No one pays for it. It is certainly not fun. It just has to be done. I remember, as a kid, I used to hate cleaning the table after a meal. So guess what is the first task I typically delegate when someone asks how they can help at home? Cleaning the table, of course. I didn't say I was a saint.

I hope it will give the kids a sense of perspective. Besides, they are bored. The summer holidays have dragged on forever and they are out of ideas. So I agree, but not before we first sit down to negotiate the terms of the agreement.

Essential, must do: A general rule of thumb, I tell them, is that we will not pay them for anything that they should do for themselves. These are daily responsibilities and are 'essential, must do'. These include taking care of their personal self and hygiene, making their beds, putting away their things like bags, clothes, shoes, books, toys, plates, cups.

Essential, nice to do: There are a few other daily tasks which are 'essential, nice to do'. These tasks are necessary for the smooth functioning of the household. Like setting or clearing the dining table, putting the clothes out to dry or folding them and so on. These are not their direct responsibility, but as members of the family, it will be nice if they help out. Again, they will not be paid for this.

Not essential, nice to do: And then there are other tasks around the house that need to be done from time to time. These fall in the bucket of 'not essential, but nice to do', like dusting, cleaning, organizing, rearranging etc. And these are the jobs for which they will be paid.

So for example, they *have* to put their plates away after a meal, but they don't *have* to clean the table every time. It would be nice if they can take turns to do it, but they won't get paid for it. If, on the other hand, they clean the kitchen cupboards or the refrigerator, they will get paid for it. I agree to the fees they ask for, anywhere between ₹10 and ₹20, depending on the difficulty of the task and the time it is likely to take.

'Can we start now?' asks my younger one, eagerly.

I hate to dampen her enthusiasm, and so I agree.

'Clean the entertainment unit and the television in *thatha's* room,' I tell her. They have been sitting in a corner and gathering dust for months.

I hand her a dusting cloth, show her how to use a bottle of Colin and leave her to her devices. Half an hour later, she calls me to come and inspect. She has done a surprisingly good job. I point out a smudge near a button and she is happy to clean it up. I hand over a ten-rupee note. She beams. Her first job. Her first pay.

We unearth an old candy box for her to store the money. We also set up a sheet for tracking the earnings and expenditures. Years ago, I remember my father using a *kanaku* book (accounting book) where he would diligently track daily expenses. And I remember doing the same once I moved to a hostel and started to manage my money, only this time using a Microsoft Excel spreadsheet. She writes down her first entry. 'Cleaned *thatha's* TV unit. ₹10.' My father would be proud of her.

'What can we do next? Clean the windows? The refrigerator? Microwave oven?' asks my older daughter.

'That's enough for today,' I insist.

They go away. Only come back to pester me again the next day, and the next day and the day after. I had not bargained for how addictive this would become. The call of money, who can resist it? I wonder if I have opened up a Pandora's Box.

⁓

Sunday afternoons are sacrosanct. It's my nap time. Two precious hours that I snatch from the demands of my life. A nap on Sunday is an 'essential, must do', a reset button that I need in order to be able to face the next week.

Today, I wake up after a refreshing nap and walk out of my bedroom. Into what looks like a glossy page out of *Good Housekeeping*. I am shocked. It is perfect. Everything is neatly arranged and in its place. Not a book or newspaper in sight. Everything is spotless. The sofa looks inviting with the plumped-up cushions, and the curtains behind it draped to fall just so. My favourite cream-coloured appliqué table cloth has been spread on the dining table, a sandalwood elephant delicately poised right in the centre of the round table. The kids excitedly pull me into the guest bedroom. The clothes have been pulled down from the clothesline, folded up and set in neat piles ready to be put away. I am amazed.

'What…' I splutter. 'How did this happen?'

'We wanted to surprise you, Amma,' they say. 'Just like that!'

The next week looks awesome already.

First Term:
June–September

From: MyKidsSchool@Bengaluru.com
To: Amma@gmail.com
Date: Friday, 29 May 2015 at 10.48 AM

        Subject: Welcome to the new term!

Dear Parent,

Greetings!

We hope the children have had a relaxing and enjoyable summer vacation.

As you are aware, the new academic session will begin on Monday, 01 June 2015. Please find attached the new bus routes and timings for the year. Do contact the office in case you have any queries regarding the same.

We are looking forward to the new term and hope to interact with you closely through the year.

With warm regards,
Principal

Her: I'm glad I'm done with 11, Amma.
Me: Why? What's the big deal about 12?
Her: One, it's not a prime number. Two, besides 1 & 12, it is divisible by four other numbers.
And three, even numbers are feminine.
There are many reasons to look forward to a birthday, but only my older daughter would have not one, but three mathematical and logical reasons.

6

Math Is Fun. Not.

I just do not *get* numbers. At all. Unlike my older daughter who simply does.

Obviously, I do know some Math. I can handle calculations. One would not expect any less after having acquired not one, but two, college degrees. I know the steps needed to solve a problem and arrive at an answer. Interest calculations, percentage growth in revenues month-on-month, cost per lead acquisition, churn rate, pie charts, bar graphs, and all such boring stuff that I deal with at work. I know what to do. Especially since I have a secret weapon in my arsenal. Microsoft Excel.

But it's a chore. A laborious, torturous chore. As excruciating as getting a root canal treatment, which I admit I have never experienced, but I have read and heard enough to know how painful they can be. If I had a choice, I would rather go to a dentist than churn numbers. I certainly do not understand how some people can look at numbers and think they are magical.

Seriously, what on earth could be fascinating about numbers? They're just, well, numbers.

To say that my older daughter is into numbers would be an understatement. Asked which famous dead personality she would like to interview for a creative writing project, she says 'Gauss! I really wish I could meet and talk with him.'

'And Gauss is….?' As is obvious, I have no clue who he is.

'A mathematician, Amma!' she says.

But, of course.

'Wouldn't you rather interview Elvis Presley or Mahatma Gandhi? You might get some interesting stories.'

'Amma, there are so many stories about Gauss. He was a child prodigy.'

'Oh?'

'One day when he was still in primary school, his teacher assigned the class a problem. The teacher thought he would give them a tough problem. He wanted to keep the kids occupied for a long time so he could take a nap! Just imagine, a teacher taking a nap in the classroom. Anyway, "Add up the numbers from one to hundred," he told the class before settling down for his nap. But Gauss found the answer in no time at all—5050. He just figured out a simple way to solve this problem without actually adding the numbers one by one. He came up with a formula. So, the sum of 1 to $n = n\ (n+1)\ /\ 2$.'

Clearly the 'King of Rock and Roll' is no match for the 'Prince of Mathematicians'.

My younger daughter is still a little young, but she too is showing distinct signs of having the same bent of mind. For example, just this morning we were doing something together, when we looked up at the clock to see what the time was. It was 12:57.

My daughter immediately said, 'Hey Amma, it's 12:57. See, $5 + 7 = 12$!'

Whereas I just said, 'It's 12:57. Time to set the table for lunch.'

∫

I. Just. Don't. Get. It.

I often see the husband and my daughters huddled together. Engrossed in one of the many puzzle books we have at home. Crouched over pieces of paper, with drawings and numbers and calculations. Solving some problem. The Bridges of Konigsberg. When is Cheryl's birthday? Making a Mobius strip. Proving Gauss's formula.

'Why are you doing this?' I ask.

'It's fun, Amma' they say casually without even lifting their head up from the paper.

I look at them, sigh and walk away.

How could solving all these problems be fun? Of what use could it be? Why do it at all? It's beyond me.

I wouldn't be caught dead doing numbers. Unless of course

if my boss wanted a report on the marketing campaign's performance, pronto. Or if it involved critical decisions such as what proportion of different flours should I use if I want to cut down the number of multigrain cookies I am baking by one third of what the recipe prescribes. Or what time should I start from home in order to reach my office for a meeting at 9 a.m., keeping in mind my steady (read: slow) driving and the inevitable Bengaluru traffic.

Talking of traffic reminds me of trains. And the dreaded train problems at school:

If a train leaves station A and travels at 60 kilometres per hour and another train leaves station B which is 90 kilometres away and travels at 45 kilometres per hour, when will they meet?

I used to hate that problem. I still do.

And there are so many variations of the train problem. Trains running in the same direction. Trains running in opposite directions. Trains crossing a stationary pole, a running man, a platform. When will they meet? Where will they meet? What is the speed? What is the distance? What is the length—of the train, of the platform in the station? It is enough to put one off trains forever.

To make matters worse, whenever my family travelled during our holidays, on those long train journeys, my father would engage us in games of, you guessed it, Math. He would point out the yellow stone kilometre markers by the side of the railway tracks and ask us to keep an eye out for them. Using our watch, we had to calculate the speed of our train and the time at which we would arrive at the next station. Meanwhile all I wanted to do was to gaze out lazily at the passing villages and spin a thousand tales in my head. Sigh.

And then there were the time and work problems:

A can finish a work in 15 days. B can do the same work in 18 days. B worked for 13 days and left the job. How many days will it take A alone to finish the work?

I had a friend who would rub his hands in glee every time our teacher brandished these time and work problems in Math class. He was the boy who always asked for more. I bet he is now a project manager in some high-tech IT company. The million dollar question though is this: Is he still rubbing his hands in glee, as he juggles customer delivery deadlines, budget constraints and people resource crunches? Ha!

But back to the husband and kids. They baffle me. It's not as if their school has given them these problems for homework. So why do they rack their brains to crack it? The problem, not the head. Could it be that they are actually having fun? But how can Math be fun?

∽

Math. A word that can send shivers down my spine. Even now. Was there ever a more dreaded subject at school?

'Amma, do you remember any algebra from school?' asks my older daughter.

'Maybe a little,' I hedge, unwilling to be pinned down. You know how it is. You want to be truthful, but you do not want to tell the whole truth either. That you remember next to nothing. That you have a recurring nightmare about recurring decimals.

'If you don't remember most of what they taught you at school, then what is the use of it?' she asks.

And therein lies the crux of the matter. What was the use

of all that teaching, if I did not learn anything?

You hear of this great divide. The have-its and the have-nots. The Math people and non-Math people. Am I one of them? The non-Math people? Numbers seem to come naturally to my daughters. Are their brains just wired that way? Or is it the way they were taught? They did go to a Montessori school where mathematical concepts were learnt by working with materials rather than direct instruction. Number rods, golden beads, spindle boxes, fraction trays and more. They could touch, feel, move things around, build it up, break it down. It was not abstract, and nor was it learnt by rote. Is that why they 'get' it? What about the husband then? He went to a conventional school, same as me. How does he 'get' it too? Is it nature or nurture?

I am unsure. And so I do what I always do, when in doubt. I turn to the Internet. I come across an insightful and superbly articulated piece by a teacher called Ben Orlin[*]. In 'The Math Ceiling: Where's your cognitive breaking point?' he talks about whether every person has a mathematical ceiling. The issue he says is not that there are 'Math people' and 'non-Math people'. Instead, he says, the issue lies in lack of understanding basic concepts. As young students we are always taught to 'do'. Steps, tips, tricks, shortcuts, roundabouts. Whatever is needed to solve a Math problem. We are taught the 'how', but there is very little time or effort spent on the 'why'. It is therefore inevitable that, with a foundation so weak, at some point the structure will come crumbling down. And that is when we end up declaring 'I hate Math'.

---

[*]http://mathwithbaddrawings.com/2015/04/08/the-math-ceiling-wheres-your-cognitive-breaking-point/

That is our ceiling, our breaking point. A point that could have been avoided, had we made an effort to address the underlying problem. Maybe as kids we did not know that there was a problem. But even as adults we do not ask the questions that will help us understand better. Simply because, as Orlin says, 'Math makes people feel stupid. It hurts to feel stupid.' So rather than confronting our fear, we simply state, 'I hate Math'. I like this guy. I wish he had taught me Math when I was younger.

A result of all this reading is that I decide I must overcome this fear, this antipathy that I have towards numbers. Maybe I will never look at numbers and think 'magic', but I could learn to like it more. Maybe even have some fun with it. So I download a game on my smartphone. An app that promises to improve my cognitive abilities through fun games that will address a lot of different skill areas like memory, speed, attention, problem-solving. The app throws up new challenges every day. It is smart too. It learns from my performance and keeps throwing me the ones I am not good at. The more I do it, the better I will get at it. It makes me calculate figures in my head, use complex logical reasoning. There are suitcases to be packed, coffee cups to be filled, birds to be followed, raindrops to be caught, train tracks to be switched, you name it. All number and logic problems cleverly camouflaged to entice me into playing the game.

I *am* excited, at first. But soon I find my mind drifting. To how the app could've been more intuitively designed, how the usability could be improved, how the rewards programme could've been better planned to avoid player dropouts and email campaigns to bring back the players day after day. Anything but the problem at hand. Occupational hazard, I'm afraid, the perils of being a digital marketer. Soon, I forget about the app.

A few weeks later when I log into the app, purely by chance, I am surprised to find that my scores have skyrocketed. It seems, the kids have been at it, using my phone to play the game to pass the time. Sigh.

∽

Needless to say, I do not help my daughters with Math. I am afraid I'll do more harm than good. That I will pass on my dread, fear and general dislike of the subject back to them. You have to be enthusiastic and passionate about a subject in order to teach it. Or at least, not actively dislike it. Kids pick up on that. They get excited when they see you so excited. It's infectious. Any attempt at faking it will not work. Besides, there is no way I could fake an interest in analysing route plans over the bridges of Konigsberg. So this is one task I actively encourage the husband to take on.

Last evening I was surprised to find my daughter engrossed in doing something with her father. She rarely goes more than ten minutes without coming to me for something or the other. But here, an entire evening had gone by without a peep from her. I was curious and went over to see what they were up to.

'I never thought Microsoft Excel could be used to do Math. I always thought it was only used to plan vacations. At least that's what Amma does,' exclaimed my daughter to her father, looking at me accusingly. She had discovered a whole new world with him, and no thanks to me.

I think back to a comment the husband had made to me in the early days of our courtship. One that I milk now for all it's worth. He said he was a 'Math cat'. I suppose he was trying to impress me. Did the thought cross my mind at that time that if we had kids, I could effectively delegate the job of Math lessons to him? Clairvoyant? Nah.

∽

This morning I caught my older daughter with a secret smile on her face.

'What is it?' I ask, curious to know what has put that beatific smile on her face.

'You know our school bus has an interesting license plate number. 153. There aren't too many numbers like it.'

'Oh?'

'If you take the cube of each of the digits and add it up, it results in the same number. So, $1 + 125 + 27 = 153$. Isn't that cool?'

So, when in doubt, I tell her what I know best. 'Go and comb your hair. It looks like a bird's nest.'

How else is one to cope? I just don't get it!

Older daughter: What a pass! That's a black-heel nutmeg.
Me: Ha, I didn't know they played football with a nutmeg.
Older daughter: Amma, stop joking. It's not funny. This is the Merseyside derby!

7

The Legion Extraordinaire

The one season that I don't particularly care for is football season. Come Premier League, my house is taken over by football fanatics. The husband and children are, to put it mildly, big fans. There is a spring in their step, a gleam in their eyes and hope burns eternal as their favourite team kicks off the new season. Weekend activities are planned around match schedules. They go out of their way to be polite and considerate to me. Subtle hints are given about an upcoming match, the unstated expectation being that my television viewing should not conflict with their match timings.

A few years back, when the local cable television provider arbitrarily blacked out league matches, the husband decided he had had enough. We would move to satellite television. I decided to keep a safe distance. The husband, who is more used to running at the measured pace of a marathon, decided to sprint. Research, quotes from service providers, package comparison, negotiation, order placement and installation—all done in under twenty-four hours. Was it because of a big match that evening? But, of course. The Merseyside derby, a fiercely fought match between long-time rivals. Wasn't it wonderful that we now had satellite television to see it?

Sometime later when I pitched for a high-end, 55-inch, flat screen, Ultra HD, LED TV (for my own selfish reasons), I should not have been surprised to meet with immediate acquiescence. What could match the pleasure of watching the game in HD with crystal clear images, every drop of sweat, every stitch on the ball, every blade of grass on the ground, seen in all its brilliant, rich, Astro Turf glory? Who would want to go to a stadium after having experienced the comfort of viewing at home, with slow motion, playback, pre-, mid-, post- and in- match analyses. And let us not forget the easy access to snacks and beverages, of the alcoholic variety for the husband and non-alcoholic variety for the children. Maybe I should have pitched for a bigger screen size or even a home theatre system for better sound effects.

∽

Early on, the husband figured out that the road to peaceful pursuit of football viewing lay in converting the children to his camp. He has done a fairly good job of brainwashing them. It all began innocently enough, with a gift. A few years ago, when the kids were perhaps eight and five, the husband returned home from a business trip abroad with a surprise for them. The kids were all over him, clamouring to see what he had bought them. Solemnly, he handed them each a package. When they unwrapped the packing, there was a reverential silence. It was red. Original Liverpool branded T-shirt and shorts, in the kids' sizes. He must've paid a fortune for it. But when it comes to the Liverpool Football Club, nothing is too much. A few months later came a calendar. Large glossy pictures capturing the players mid-shot in gravity defying positions. The kids could now identify the players. Soon, he was showing them video clips of exciting goals. And just like that they were hooked to the game.

Today, given a choice between watching a movie and watching a match, they will actually pick the match. I guess I need to up my game, pun intended. The road to Bollywood potboilers begins with sports movies. Maybe I should start with *Lagaan*, *Chak de! India* and *Bend it Like Beckham*, and then gradually lead them into the rest. There's time to convert them yet. Or, is there?

In the meanwhile, I play the devil's advocate.

'Why do you support the Liverpool Football Club? They are not doing too well.'

'Amma just because they are having a bad run this season doesn't mean we should ditch them.'

'Don't you think you should check out the other teams before you decide which team to support? Maybe Manchester United or Chelsea?'

I get a stony glare, one that says 'Don't be ridiculous Amma'. Their father is a Liverpool fan and so are they. That's all there is to it. They are 'The Reds'.

We are lucky. With the time zones being what they are, the matches are inevitably telecast in the evenings and occasionally late at night. The children often stay up late to watch the matches. If it is a school day the next day and they have to turn in early, they set the match to record, to be savoured later. On such days, their first question on waking up is, 'Appa, who won? What was the score?' My older daughter pores over the newspapers, scrutinizing the table for points and positions. Who moved up, who moved down, what are the odds. She studies the match reports with such intensity as if she might have a test on it the next day.

It is quite amusing to see all this fuss about a game. They look quite silly, grown men in shorts and unfashionable long socks, running around a ball, come sun, rain, or even occasionally, hail. Going by the fervour, it is nothing less than a religion, at whose altar the fans worship. So weekend after weekend, my family plonk themselves down, with banners held up in front of the television screen, dressed identically, my red brigade. Go Red!

They are quite vocal and aggressive too, in their support. There are loud cheers, high fives, fist pumps, impatient sighs, and to my surprise, even jeering. It's a war out there and all is fair in love and football. And so I learn the following valuable lessons, unwritten rules in the true football fan's handbook:

1. If our team wins, that is to be expected. We are *the* best.
2. If our team loses, the referee was biased.
3. If a new player joins the team, he is probably good, otherwise we wouldn't pick him.
4. If a player leaves the team, good riddance, especially

because he was to blame for the bad season.
5. And if that player who left happens to play against us as a part of the opposing team, boo him!

There's more along these lines.

I usually stay away when these matches are on. They are intense affairs. The husband has a glazed look in his eyes. He is in the zone. My older daughter has a dozen questions to ask, especially of the hypothetical sort.

'Appa, what would happen if team A draws team B, but team C beats team D who is ahead of team A in penalties?'

If this, then what? If that, then what? He is alternately indulgent and impatient. It all depends on how Liverpool is playing that day. My younger daughter is less involved. She is even known to doze off from time to time. If I dare suggest that she go sleep in her bed, she insists vehemently, 'I'm watching the game Amma'.

If I do stay, occasionally I am treated to an impromptu lesson. I learn about the back-heel nutmeg, for instance. My daughters tell me that the nutmeg is when a player plays the ball through the legs of the opponent. In this move, the player pulls the ball back towards himself to fool the opponent into stepping closer. When the opponent moves his legs, the player passes the ball through it. It is called a back-heel nutmeg when this move is done using the heel.

It turns out this whole back-heel nutmeg routine is a sleight of the leg. This phrase actually has some interesting stories surrounding its origins including one involving the crown jewels. But the story that interests me is the one about the nutmeg trade between England and America. Apparently, nutmegs were such a valuable commodity that traders often pulled a fast one by including fake wooden nutmegs in the stock. So being 'nutmegged' meant that someone had been tricked.

In addition to impromptu lessons, I am also treated to the occasional trivia. For example, did you know that in seven of the last ten Football World Cup finals, at least two players shared a birthday? Or that in the entire history of the Football World Cups, at least three of them have had a pair of twins playing in them?

When the I-League, India's professional football league, and the newly formed Bengaluru Football Club started to gain some prominence recently, no one was more enthused than my family. They now had a home team that they could cheer for. When I found out that the team was nicknamed 'The Blues', I asked my kids if this didn't conflict with 'The Reds'. They chose the high road. They decided to ignore me and focus instead on the fact that 'The Blues' were in excellent form. There is now talk of buying season tickets for home matches.

∽

I look forward to off-season. But in the absence of football, there is always something else. Like cricket or tennis.

'I don't like Nadal', I say.

My daughters are shocked. I don't know whether it is because I have faulted their hero or because I actually have an opinion on such matters.

'Why?' they ask.

'His hair is too long and it's so messy,' I say perversely.

There is much eye-rolling as the kids return to watching the match.

'Why doesn't he get it cut?' I add. That's the extent of my contribution to the game.

'Amma, forget his hair and watch the match,' commands my older daughter.

Discussions such as this are right up my younger one's alley though. She takes the bait. 'What about Shikhar Dhawan's moustache or Virat Kohli's earring Amma, what do you think about that?'

There is hope for this kid.

For such big sports fans, you would think my kids would also enjoy playing. But no, my children belong to the legion of sports fans. They are happy to enjoy it from the comfort of their home. Cricket, football, tennis, badminton, kabaddi, you name it, they follow it. I try to push them out of the house every evening, encouraging them to go and play. But it is half-hearted, at best. Because I was the same growing up. I liked staying at home. I vastly preferred standing at the balcony and looking down upon my fiefdom. I had a vivid imagination even then.

As cities grow, it is becoming harder and harder for children to find the space they need to play. The community I live in and others that I see around me have tried to carve out play areas. Often though, walkways and side streets turn into cricket pitches. Badminton is played on front porches with the gate serving as the net. There is a tennis court which doubles up as a football ground in the evenings. With strict time slots for different age groups. So many rules, so many restrictions. Add to that the burden of homework, tuition classes and extracurricular activities. Who has time to play anymore?

It is yet another Sunday evening. Yet another match. 'This is so boring, nothing exciting ever happens,' I grumble. So my older daughter decides to tell me a story:

The year was 1996. The day, Sunday, 20 March. It was a few months before the Football World Cup. The Jules Rimet Trophy, which is awarded to the winner, was on display at a public stamp exhibition at Westminster Central Hall. Around noon, suddenly, the trophy disappeared. There was a lot of security, and yet nobody knew how it was stolen. So Scotland Yard was called in. What happened thereafter was nothing short of a drama. The Chairman of the Football Association received an anonymous call. This was followed by a ransom demand of £15,000. The police made arrangements for the ransom exchange. False paper money was hurriedly put together. At the exchange, a car chase ensued and soon the offender was nabbed. But he turned out to be just the middleman. The real culprit and the trophy were still nowhere to be found.

Seven days later, Pickles, a mixed breed collie, was taking a walk with his owner David Corbett, in the Beulah Hill district of South London. He suddenly came across a package in a garden hedge. It was wrapped in newspaper. He nudged it. He sniffed at it. Then he let out an excited bark. Turns out Pickles had accidentally stumbled upon the missing trophy. That year England went on to win the World Cup and Pickles became a national hero. Not to mention his owner pocketed a tidy sum as reward money.

I was charmed. Who knew there was a story, a whodunnit no less with all that drama, to be found in football? They might make a convert out of me after all.

> Her: Amma, what are we having for dinner?
> Me (in my best American drawl): Mildly spiced pancakes made from coarsely ground garbanzo beans, pigeon peas and rice. Served with a topping of lightly sautéed shallots and greens. And a huge dollop of butter just for you!
> For the uninitiated, that's adai dosa.

8

If It's Dinner, It Must Be Dosa

At a party, I am introduced to another mom. She lives in the US and is visiting her in-laws' home in Bengaluru for the holidays. She has a son, about seven years old. I ask her how he is getting along at his grandparents' home, and I am hit with the mother-in-law of all grouses.

'How can you eat dosa every day? How can that be healthy for kids?' She is a Punjabi, married to a Tamilian. 'You know, my mother-in-law, she makes dosa for dinner. Every. Single. Day.'

'For Tamilians, the dosa is like your roti. Don't you eat roti every day?' I ask her.

'Of course not!' she says, offended. 'I put in a lot of effort to plan every single meal. I make sure every food group is covered in every meal.'

'Oh yes, the food pyramid,' I say knowledgeably.

'No, no. That is old news. In the US we have moved from the food pyramid to the food plate. It's now a round plate with portions for carbs, proteins, veggies and fruits and a side helping of dairy. I follow that now.'

'Triangle, circle…soon they'll run out of shapes,' I joke, rather lamely.

'You know, I put in so much effort and here my mother-in-law just serves my son dosa,' she says, in a huff. 'I *never* repeat a meal. Especially not dinner. As educated parents, isn't it our job to serve nutritious and diverse food at every mealtime for our children? I bet you are the same. What do you do for dinner?'

'Err, dosa…'

In our house, if it's dinner it must be dosa. Plain dosa, set dosa, ghee roast, podi dosa, onion dosa, masala dosa, adai dosa, *muzhu uzhundu* dosa, appam, *rava* dosa, *godumai* dosa, *kothammali* dosa, *neer* dosa… Before you go thinking that my house is the veritable Sathya Sagar Darshini restaurant, let me assure you that while the options are endless, my offerings are not always. Ok, I confess. I make three, maybe four of those varieties on a regular basis.

To tell you the truth, the whole conversation at the party bothered me. It's not that I am a dosa fanatic. If anything, I have a vivid memory of stating quite haughtily to my then new husband many years ago that I was not your 'typical South Indian'. How the mighty have fallen. While I am not likely to wax eloquent about the sublime culinary experience that is the dosa, I do object to others casting aspersions on it. The much maligned dosa is so much more. At the very least, it is a perfectly balanced meal. The dosa batter made from rice and dal covers two food groups—carbohydrates and proteins. Add in the sambar or the chutney—you have an additional portion of protein and the choicest pickings when it comes to the veggies. Ghee on the dosa for the kids? You can tick dairy off the list. And let's not forget the always-in-stock, freshly imported once every two weeks from my mother's house, *milagai podi*, or gunpowder as it is commonly known. Lazy to resort to gunpowder, you say? I like to think of it as initiating my kids' palates to complex, mature flavours.

'Those poor kids,' you must be thinking. Before you go sympathizing with my certainly not poor or traumatized kids, let me reassure you, I do rustle up the occasional soup and pasta, noodles, quesadilla, *idiyappam*, *pav bhaaji* or *dhokla* for some variety during the week.

But for my kids, nothing can come close to the 'good life'. Having grown up on a staple diet of Enid Blytons, for them, the good life means boarding schools, horses, picnics and tea with buttered scones, marmalade and cake. Not for them is the local Kissan mixed-fruit jam or the thickly sliced milk bread from the local bakery. On a recent holiday in London we decided to treat the kids to the original buttered scones and marmalade. There was a lot of excitement and much elbowing to get that first bite.

'It's not fair that she should get the first helping just because she is younger.'

'So what if she is older? Why should she be the first in everything?'

Just as I settled the bickering by slicing the scone in half, the pushing began again. This time they were pushing the plate back, rushing to offer it to the other.

'You have it…', 'No you have it…', 'No you…'.

The marmalade, it seemed, was too bitter, the scones too buttery.

My daughter summed it up best when she said, 'I would rather have dosa, Amma.'

So much for the good life.

༄

While my older daughter absolutely loves dosa, the younger one is not always quite so enthusiastic. She is even known to register a protest occasionally. I do have a few tricks up my sleeve to deal with just these kind of situations. When she asks me what's for dinner, I put on my best American drawl and say with as much flourish as I can muster:

'Today we have light fluffy crepes, served with your choice of sweet saffron milk or exotic vegetables in delicately spiced coconut curry'. That's appam, with sweet milk or vegetable stew.

Or:

'Thick, soft pancakes topped with lightly sautéed shallots. Served with a mélange of softly cooked vegetables simmered in a delicate, savoury, lentil broth.' Onion uttappam and sambar.

She is delighted and distracted. And that takes care of dinner.

With dosas on her mind, my older daughter tells me she has picked cuisine for a project at school. Her class is studying the Roman Empire this term. Their project is to research some aspect of the Roman Empire and turn in a report.

'But what's the big deal with Roman food? Surely all they

ate were cabbage stew and roast boar?' I ask.

'Amma, the Asterix comics are not the gold standard for ancient Roman cuisine,' she says.

'But why food?' I ask. Why not pick culture, architecture, attire, even mythology, at which the kid is admittedly a bigger expert than I could ever hope to be, thanks to Rick Riordan.

'The Romans had gastronomic gumption,' she states, momentarily delighted with her own ability to alliterate. 'I wonder if they had anything like dosas. I think it would be interesting to know what their food was like and what ingredients they used back then. And it would be fun to make and take some samples to school, and share it with my friends.'

So begins our search for recipes on the Internet. There's Cato's Roman Bread. Seems simple enough. Flour, olive oil, salt, water. Oh wait, it needs 'spelt flour'. I have never heard of spelt flour. Apparently it belongs to the wheat family. Same genus, different species. It's light, nutritious and has a nutty flavour. It used to be cultivated by ancient civilizations around eight thousand years ago. It has now made a comeback of sorts in the form of health food, although where can one get it in Bengaluru is anybody's guess.

So here's the question. If I make Roman bread with regular wheat flour and no one hears about it, will it still be Roman bread? Apparently not, according to my daughter.

We move on to the next recipe. This one requires lovage seeds. *Ajwain*? We wonder. Alas, no. Wikipedia tells us that *ajwain* is often mistaken for lovage seeds. But *ajwain* is, in fact, carom seeds or bishop's weed. As for lovage seeds, we still have no idea what they are.

We move on to the next recipe. This one requires rue. We

learn it is the national herb of Lithuania, but that's neither here nor there. Even if we do manage to get it in some organic store, this recipe calls for fish sauce. Anywhere else in the world, fish would probably be considered vegetarian food. But we know better, don't we? So that's the end of that recipe.

By now we are tired and hungry, and we decide it is probably a good idea to table this project for now.

'Shall we eat?' I ask her. 'What do you want for dinner?'

'Today I feel like having some comfort food, Amma.'

'What would you like to have?'

'Can you give me some crispy crêpes served with a topping of lightly sautéed shallots?' she asks.

I look at her blankly.

'Amma, I'm just asking for onion dosa,' she says with a mischievous twinkle in her eye. 'If it's dinner, it must be dosa, right?'

> 'Sometimes I wonder what it would be like if we were lice.
> Imagine living in someone's head. A clump of hair
> would be like a galaxy and we'd all be
> crawling around in our own world.'
> —Bedtime musings of my daughter
> with an overactive imagination

9

In Which We Talk about Something Embarrassing

What is it with little girls and lice? They seem to have a childhood long love affair with them. Lanky hair, wavy hair, limp hair, springy hair, long hair, short hair. It does not matter, for these creepy crawlies seem to move with their claw-like legs from one head onto another with no discrimination. All the lather from the anti-lice shampoo brought hurriedly from the local *kirana* store, will not get rid of them.

'Amma, why are you getting annoyed?' asks my older

daughter. I have been eyeing my younger one, my brows furrowed, as she scratches her head.

'If one of you gets it, the other is sure to get it too,' I reply. *And me too*, although I don't say that out loud.

'Yes, she is the generous sort,' says my cheeky older daughter. 'She likes to share everything.'

'That is so lame,' shoots back my spirited younger daughter.

'No it's not. If they are crawling, they can't be lame,' guffaws my older daughter, always happy to get the last word in.

∽

I am a nitpicking mom. Literally. Weekend mornings will find me going through the elaborate ritual of first oiling my daughters' hair, then combing through it, scouring for nits and lice. I almost feel like I have won a battle, when I manage to snag one in the teeth of the comb, then carefully manoeuvre it out from between the teeth on to the base of the comb, and kill it. Call me bloodthirsty if you will, but nothing is quite as satisfying as squashing a squirming louse firmly with the thumbnail. Unfortunately, though the battle may be won, the war is not. No sooner do I crush all that I can lay my hands on this week that others take their place.

Lice. They are enough to make one cringe with embarrassment. What could be more mortifying than your child being caught scratching their head? As mothers, we instantly feel responsible, as if our parenting abilities are responsible. The guilt. Fathers, at least the ones I am acquainted with, don't seem to care much.

Why are we so embarrassed about lice? Studies have

repeatedly shown that personal hygiene and cleanliness of the surroundings have nothing to do with getting head lice. There is nothing disgusting or dirty associated with them. And yet, that is exactly how head lice is perceived. A family friend, a doctor by profession, assures me that head lice are not known to spread disease. This is a scientifically proven fact. They might be a bother, what with all the itching and scratching, which can at times lead to rashes. But they are certainly not a medical or health hazard, unlike cockroaches, which we seem to be more comfortable talking about in public. It is quite common to find friends swapping phone numbers of pest control vendors and tips on home remedies.

'You must mix flour with baking soda and sugar, make little balls and leave them around the kitchen. The roaches will vanish overnight,' says a friend.

'Try Laxman Rekha,' says my mother, who swears by this little chalk stick to keep the cockroaches at bay.

There is much sympathetic tsk-ing and head shaking. It seems there is no shame in admitting to having cockroaches in your home. But lice on your child's head? One definitely does not admit to their existence. At least not in public.

While there are no exact figures, studies seem to indicate that the problem is more common among girls than boys, maybe because of more frequent head-to-head contact. You have only to see cousins and friends playing and giggling together to know that this is true. Was it just my imagination that I recently caught my brother giving me 'the look'? His toddler had ended up with a few lice on her head after playing with my kids. My mother tried to hesitantly broach the matter, with subtle hints that I might want to keep a closer eye on the kids' heads. I swiftly changed the topic. After all my kids too had been known to catch quite a few from their older cousins. What's a few lice between cousins?

Talking of friends, a few years ago, one of mine received an urgent phone call from the school. Her daughter was a young kid in primary school in the United States. At first she panicked, not knowing what to think. Only, it was worse, much worse. The school nurse had found lice on her daughter's head. The parents were asked to come and pick up their daughter immediately. They were strictly instructed not to send her back till her head was all clear. Needless to say, my friend and her husband were flustered. Who had ever heard of lice being a cause for, what seemed like, suspension from school?

Schools in developed countries like the United States and the United Kingdom unfortunately take quite a harsh view on this matter. They have 'no-nit' policies, which require kids to be completely free of lice, eggs and nits, before they can go back to school. This, in spite of the fact that several government bodies and associations now recommend that 'no-nit' policies should be discontinued.

∽

Back home, fully convinced that this whole problem has originated at school, I instruct my daughters not to play with their heads so close to their friends. When I visit their school, I watch their friends like a hawk. Who is scratching their head? Who is spreading the lice? Who is the culprit? Not that I plan to do anything once I find out. But it is good to know such things. I look around. I catch another mother's eye, and start to smile, only to suddenly stop short. It only just occurs to me that she is, in fact, giving me 'the look', for she has seen my daughter scratching her head.

I make a firm resolution. No more sticking my head in the sand. I shall be beyond reproach. I will redouble my efforts. Work tirelessly towards the eradication of lice in my home.

A cousin, hearing of my travails with the ineffective plastic combs, gets us a traditional wooden comb bought from one of the 'Fancy' shops in the by-lanes of Chennai. But much like chopsticks, I am unable to get a proper grip. Another tells me about a medicated shampoo that has worked well for her kids. Yet another cousin gets us a 'complete' lice and nit elimination kit from the US. There is a lice-killing shampoo, a nit comb-out gel, a long metal lice comb, a fine-tooth nit comb, a cleaning brush, and even a magnifying glass. I set up the paraphernalia one Sunday morning and get to work. I follow the instructions diligently. Surprise, it works. And no squashing each and every squirming louse with my thumbnail either. Surely that's good news. Isn't it? But it doesn't last. Alas, a month later, much like Arnold Schwarzenegger, they are back. Since I am not in favour of using chemical treatments on the kids at such frequent intervals I decide to keep the metal combs and shelve the rest of the kit.

I get on to the Internet to find some other solutions. I search for 'How to remove lice'. There are only about 5.7 million results. They go down to about one million when I narrow my search to home remedies. I try the most popular suggestion.

Vinegar. This one is easily available at home. While it has no effect on the adult lice, apparently the acetic acid in vinegar is quite effective on nits. It dissolves the layer that glues the nits to the hair. Once loosened, it is fairly easy to remove with a comb. My daughters, initially eager to try out something new, soon wrinkle up their noses in disgust. They hate the smell of vinegar and want me to wash it off immediately. The recommended waiting time is one hour. I cajole them into holding on for a while, but it doesn't last. So we wash it off. Within that short period though, we seem to have had some success. I am hopeful. But the kids have a different idea. 'Never again!' they state quite firmly.

Next on the list is mouthwash. This one they like better. My younger daughter starts wondering what it would be like if we were lice living on someone's head. Something in the menthol must have set off her already overactive imagination. This is a thought that fascinates her to no end and keeps popping up at the oddest of times. But besides such random musings, nothing much else really happens. So we move on to the next one in the list.

Mayonnaise. Death by suffocation. The kids are aghast. They refuse to even let me contemplate this method. 'Amma, how could you? It is cruel!' they say and that is the end of the discussion.

So it is back to the basics.

'Girls, can you come here?' I call out.

'Amma, not again,' they whine when they see me brandishing a bottle of coconut oil and the nit comb.

But I refuse to give in. The next generation army of lice has risen and there is yet another battle to be waged this week. My fingers are tingling. I am ready. One louse at a time, one louse at a time.

'Appa, you should hear Amma when she drives. "Look at that guy! Idiot! He doesn't know how to drive! Just look at him! Idiot! Didn't he learn how to use the indicator? Idiot! Can't he see that the signal is still red? Idiot!" She gets so worked up. It's quite funny.'

10

Mind Your Language

If there is one superhero I would like to be, it would be Phantom, The Super Babe (aka The Ghost Who Walks the Road). I would even take the Oath of the Skull: 'I swear to devote my life to the destruction of traffic offenders in all their forms, and my daughters and their daughters shall follow me.' Kapow!

I imagine myself zipping through the streets of Bengaluru. Sans the skin-tight suit. Sadly there is no superhuman power that could possibly help me carry off a skintight suit. One touch of my skull ring, and there goes the traffic offender's driver's license. Ran the red light? Zap! Reckless overtaking? Zap! No indicators? Zap! Parallel parking on a busy road? Zap! Holding up traffic at a crossing? Impatient honking? Going too fast? Going too slow? Zap! Zap! Zap! And Zap!

I would make the world, or at least Bengaluru, a better place if only I could obliterate two-thirds of the driver's licenses in the city. They might even give me a Best Citizen Award.

I admit it. I get quite worked up about traffic. I spend a fair bit of time carting my kids around, to and fro from all the different classes they go to. Keyboard, guitar, swimming, dance, art and craft... I am the veritable soccer mom. Only my kids don't play soccer. But then, you already know that.

If you have ever driven on the roads of Bengaluru, you would know just how frustrating it is. There is only one rule of the road—'Break every rule!' I have so many vile thoughts and curses running through my head. But with the kids in the backseat, I restrict myself to one or two or five deeply felt 'Idiots'. It's a wonder my brain doesn't turn putrid and decompose, what with all those expletives piled up.

So yes, I would love to be Phantom, The Super Babe. Sadly, I don't see my daughters following my footsteps. My younger daughter is prone to chiding me: 'Amma please don't use bad words' (if only she knew). Meanwhile, my older daughter looks on, secretly amused to see her mother unravel, and silently files away the tirade, to be treacherously giggled over with her father later. Tsk, tsk.

∫

Speaking of *bad words*, it is quite distressing to see that they are so common, especially among kids these days. A walk through the playground is enough to turn your ears red. There are profanities flying all around you. Crude words, rude gestures. I used to think that this was not my problem, or at least that it would become my problem only once my kids became teenagers. Until I started hearing otherwise from my younger daughter.

'Amma, what does it mean when someone shows you their middle finger?'

'A girl in the bus called my friend dumb-face.'

'One boy in my class used the F-word, Amma. And another one used the A-word.'

The S-word...the B-word...the M-word... Sigh. Is there any letter left at all?

Much as I would like to protect my daughters, it is inevitable that they hear and see things I would rather they didn't. The first time I heard a swear word coming from my four-year-old, the F-word, no less, I almost had a heart attack. On probing, it turned out she had no idea it was a bad word, much less what it meant. She had heard some kids use it repeatedly in the playground and was just parroting it. Children seem to have a special radar when it comes to zoning in on forbidden words.

So we talk about it often at home. I tell my daughters that people who use bad words do so because they think it is cool. But what's so cool about using the same few foul words for every situation? They probably don't have the power of a good vocabulary to express themselves and so they resort to such words. 'You have such a fabulous vocabulary, and that's so cool,' I tell them. 'Take pride in it and use it.'

I tell them how attractive it is to hear somebody use *proper* English. I have a weakness for men who use formal English, more so when it is peppered with typical British wit and humour. Understated and self-deprecatory. Think Sherlock Holmes in the

TV series. Benedict Cumberbatch or Jonny Lee Miller, either one will do. Or Colin Firth in any one of his many period films. Or *Downton Abbey*. You might roll your eyes. I know my kids would. All these are reel characters and they are set in an era long gone. But I can be quite old-fashioned that way.

This is perhaps the only occasion on which I will admit to being anything that has the word 'old' in it.

> Me: You need to do more around the house.
> Her: I answer the phone... I answer the door... I even answer you back, Amma!

11

Tongue-in-Cheek

My younger daughter has been thinking a lot about words lately. This morning as I was busy folding clothes, she came up to me with a question.

'Amma, what was my first word?'

'Hmmm, let me think. Mum mum,' I said.

'You mean my first word was you?' she asked eagerly.

'No' I said. 'You used to call your food "mum mum".'

'Oh!'

I think she was a wee bit disappointed that her first word was food and not her mother. To tell you the truth, one could be forgiven for mistaking the 'mum mum' to mean mom or Amma as she calls me now. She was, after all, more or less glued to my side for the first five years of her life. She certainly showed her preference in action if not in words.

Like most new parents, I remember being captivated by all the gibberish that both my daughters spouted as babies. Even when their 'words' were unintelligible and their 'talk' made no sense, I knew exactly what they were saying. I was so fascinated and couldn't wait for them to grow up and start talking. Properly. So we could have long, meaningful conversations.

They did grow up and learn to talk. Their vocabulary expanded by leaps and bounds. But what I did not expect or bargain for was the cheekiness that came with it. The sassy retorts. The general impudence and irreverence.

∫

Is it just my kids? Growing up, I could not imagine making fun of my parents. I still can't. But my kids routinely pull our legs. They make fun of their father's hair. My age. His forgetfulness. My fussiness. His lame jokes. My vanity. In fact, nothing seems to be off limits.

They are pretty free with their expert comments and comebacks on everything. Being the only parent around during most of their waking hours, I am usually at the receiving end of such generosity.

My older daughter is slightly prone to seriousness. Her sense of humour has been slow in developing. Or perhaps I am the one who has been slow in realizing that she has one. In any case, she has a wicked sense of humour and often dead-pans sly comments with a completely straight face, catching you by surprise, leaving you to wonder, 'Did she really…?'

Sometime back, my brother was visiting us in Bengaluru. The indulgent uncle that he is, he bought my kids, among other things, a working model of a helicopter. My daughters were excited with the prospect of flying their own helicopter. My older daughter immediately took control of the remote. In no time at all, she had figured out the controls and had the helicopter up in the air. My younger daughter happily skipped along, chasing the helicopter from room to room.

'Fly low, *kanna*. It's safer,' I urged my older daughter as she kept flying higher and higher so it would be just out of her sister's reach.

'Amma, you have to get high if you want to have fun!'

Did she really...?

My younger daughter, on the other hand, was born with her tongue firmly in cheek. Droll humour, lame jokes, witty puns, cheeky retorts, she loves them all and dishes them out with relish. Should the tables be turned, she is just as unflustered and doesn't easily get offended or upset. Like her father, she loves pulling my leg. Only, unlike her father, she does it fearlessly.

The other day, I asked her to help me set the table. In no time at all, she was done.

'You didn't set a place for me? You forgot me!' I said in mock outrage. And then milking the tragedy for all its worth, I said, 'How could you forget me? What would you do without me, your Amma, the Great?'

'I've heard that the thing that makes people great is their modesty.' The kid's knack for repartee is unfortunately way better than mine for drama.

'Oh yeah? Well, you should forget about what you heard. Instead, you should listen to me. I do know more,' I said, falling back on my haughty Amma-knows-best voice.

To which, pat came her reply.

'Yes Amma, I know. *Old* people are wiser.'

Ouch.

⌁

If I can't seem to get the upper hand in any conversation with my kids, the husband fares no better. Commenting about his hair or lack thereof is one of their favourite pastimes. His ever-expanding 'cricket pitch'. That's what they call his bald spot.

'Why do people lose hair, Appa?' asks my older daughter.

'As you lose hair, you become more civilized,' he says, only half-seriously. 'Think apes and then think humans. See how far we've come.'

'You've got a moustache and I haven't. Now who's more civilized?' she guffaws.

Round one to the girls.

Now that my older daughter is almost as tall as me, her fondest wish is that she should outshoot her father as well.

'I hope I will be taller than you, Appa,' she says hopefully.

'Men in general are taller than women,' he says kindly.

'And women, in general are smarter than men, Appa,' says my younger daughter, smirking.

Fist bumps and giggles all around as the grossly outnumbered and outsmarted Appa concedes yet another round.

The poor man, he never seems to have the final word in anything with the kids these days. When I commiserate with him, he raises his eyebrows and giving me a pointed look, he says, 'Only the kids?'

Second Term:
October–December

From: MyKidsSchool@Bengaluru.com
To: Amma@gmail.com
Date: Mon, 05 October 2015 at 11.52 AM

Subject: Second Term—Bird watching session for Junior school

Dear Parent,

Greetings!

In the second term, as a part of their ongoing Environmental Sciences module on birds, the children of junior school will have birdwatching sessions in school on 13 and 14 October 2015.

The children will come to school by their regular buses on Tuesday, 13 October and will stay back in school. They will return on Wednesday, 14 October after school by the school buses as usual. Please find attached a list of things they need to carry for this activity and their overnight stay at the school.

With warm regards,
Principal

'Amma, you know, now that I think about it, what a *wild* school we have. And wild children too!'
says my younger daughter recounting her
close encounters with the animal kind.

12

Pet Peeves

'Amma, which do you like more, cats or dogs?' asks my older daughter.

I have just picked her up from her evening class and as we walk back to the car, we pass half a dozen dogs on their evening walk. There is a little runt of a dog, almost hanging off the leash, an aging Alsatian barely shuffling along, a frisky Pomeranian, and a cute little pug which makes my daughter go 'awwww'. There are three or four stray dogs in a pack that prance around, barking excitedly, but they keep a safe distance on seeing the sticks that the owners carry to keep them at bay. There is also a huge hulk of a dog whose breed I cannot quite identify. Perhaps it is a Great Dane. It is almost as big as a calf and even ambles like one. A cat streaks out from under our car just as I open the door.

'So Amma, which one do you like more, cats or dogs?'

'Neither,' I reply.

'But why?'

'I just don't like them or want them near me.'

'But why?'

'Maybe it's because I am scared of them.'

'You know, they are probably more scared of you than you are of them,' she says quite astutely.

'That may be true, but we are still not getting you a pet,' I tell her giving her a pointed look. She laughs. Oops, caught, but I guess it was worth a try, says her grin.

That's what this whole conversation has been all about. Pets. From as far back as I can remember, the girls have wanted a pet. And I have not. We all have our pet peeves. And mine are pets. And messy rooms, shaggy hair, cold weather, being late…it's a long list, but let's just say that pets rank high on my list of pet peeves. I have never ever wanted to have pets. This is the one thing on which the husband and I are in complete agreement. Or at least I think he agrees with me. If he doesn't, he has been wise enough to keep that opinion to himself.

'Amma, can we get a pet?' is a question that keeps popping up quite regularly in our house.

And my answer to that is always a resounding 'No'.

'Why not?'

'I don't want to have pets. I've got you two and that's quite enough for me, thank you.'

'Are you saying we are animals?'

'I didn't say that. You did.' I grin.

They are not amused. They are also not ones to give up so easily.

'How about a hamster? Or a rabbit?' they plead. 'They are small and cute and cuddly.'

'No.'

'How about birds? Actually no, let's not get birds. It is too cruel to keep them confined in a cage. How about a dog?'

'No.'

'But why not?'

'You can get a pet once you are older and are living on your own.'

'But why not now?'

'Because I have enough of a job taking care of you two. I don't want to add to my work by getting a dog.'

I don't know where it comes from, this fascination that my daughters have for pets. Maybe it is all the Enid Blytons they have read. No adventure is complete without a dog following the kids around. Maybe it's not just my daughters and all kids are fascinated by pets. Or maybe it's all thanks to their school.

While we live in the heart of Bengaluru city, my daughters go to a school that is located on the outskirts, in a valley, in the middle of a verdant forest. When asked what her favourite subject is, my younger daughter says 'Nature Walk'. Occasionally, they stay overnight at school to go birdwatching early in the mornings. They are even known to climb trees.

A few months after she first started school, one day my daughter came home drenched from waist down.

'What happened?' I asked, taken aback.

'I was leaning over to look at a frog in the guppy fishpond and I fell in, Amma,' she said quite pleased with herself.

In their school, toppling into the one-foot deep pond is almost a rite of passage. The valley is home to many species of birds, insects, reptiles and mammals. There are monkeys and dogs aplenty. And other animals that I prefer not to think or know about. Until the school newsletter pops up in my email box with news about panther and elephant sightings, and pictures of cobras coiled up in the bathrooms. I almost have a heart attack.

I ask the children about it. The cobras and elephants are old news, they say. But yes, there have been panther sightings recently. Forest officials have been consulted and the school has chalked out several safety measures. Metal *dabbas* or boxes have been hung upside down with sticks attached to them at regular intervals along the forest pathways. The children have been instructed to always walk in groups and beat upon the boxes to scare off the animals, should they catch sight of one. The children and the teachers have had long discussions about why this is happening, the impact of commercialization as man encroaches upon nature.

They are calm. Unlike me. I am uneasy, filled with trepidation. But in a few months, the panther too becomes old news and they are back to talking about Apple snails and African snails, red-whiskered bulbuls and Tickell's blue flycatchers. And pets.

'Amma, my friend's dog just had some puppies and she offered one to me,' says my older daughter as soon as she gets out of the school bus one evening.

'Well, you know what the answer is.'

'Yeah. You don't want to add to your work by getting a dog,' she says, quoting me verbatim.

'But it won't be much work, Amma,' says my younger one.

'Oh no? At least you kids are toilet-trained,' I say and they giggle at this. 'But a puppy? Who'll clean up after it? I don't want the responsibility.'

'Amma, we'll do it. We'll take care of everything.'

'Oh yeah? Like the fish?'

The fish. Remember the one that my daughter received as a return gift at a birthday party she attended? Given my stand on pets, the obvious thing to do at that time would've been to refuse the gift. But I did the polite thing instead and we brought the fish home. It was a small fish and it came in a really tiny tank. The girls were very excited. They kept bickering for a day over what they would name it. They finally settled upon 'Jade'.

'What kind of a name is Jade? Why can't you call it Kayilvizhi?' asked the husband wiggling his eyebrows. He has a penchant for everything Tamil, especially names. Given a choice he would've named at least one of our daughters Balathirupurasundari. *Ball-a-thirupura-sundari*. Beauty who can turn the ball. Or, beautiful bowler. My daughters have a lot to thank me for. The name Kayilvizhi, in comparison, is quite tame. It means fish-eyed in Tamil.

'Appa...stop it!' groaned the girls.

So Jade it was.

The first few days, the kids spent a long time watching Jade swim about. They layered the bottom of the tank with little pebbles and coloured marbles. They fought over who would feed the fish and help me with cleaning the tank. A couple of weeks later though, the fish lay forgotten. Every day the husband's first question when he walked in through the door would be. 'Have you fed the fish?' The answers ranged from yes, no, I don't remember, to I thought 'she' fed it. He would often tsk, tsk over the sorry state of the fish tank. Sensing an opportunity, I successfully handed over the task of cleaning the little tank to the husband. I think out of all of us, he was the most attached to the fish. This, in spite of it not being named a proper Tamil name.

A few months later, we went on a two-week long holiday leaving Jade under my parents' care. When we came back we had a big surprise waiting for us. Jade had new digs. A big rectangular tank with a bright blue sloping roof and a fancy oxygen pump. My parents had felt sorry for Jade in its tiny tank. So they bought a new, much bigger tank and justified the purchase saying that they intended to get the kids more fish. However, they had forgotten that Jade was a Betta fish and the Betta are fighter fish. You have to keep them away from the other fish, else they will kill them. So Jade continued to swim about in solitary splendour in its new abode.

This lasted all of two weeks before Jade quietly passed on to fish heaven. And the fish tank moved to sit empty in the loft.

I am shaken out of my reminiscences and brought back to the present by the sound of the girls whispering excitedly.

'If you are still talking about the puppy your friend wanted to give you, the answer is still no.'

'No Amma, forget about pets. We know they are a lot of work,' they say.

'Oh?'

'Listen, we have a brilliant idea.'

I look at them suspiciously.

'Why don't you and Appa have another baby instead? Now that would be awesome.'

A baby!

Her: Amma, I didn't realize you had so many grey hairs on your head!

Me: And guess who contributed the most?

13

Aap Kaunse College Mein Ho? (Which College Do You Study in?)

My daughters have got babies on their minds. Cute, cuddly, adorable babies. Everywhere we look, we see babies. We've just made a trip to Chennai and met a cousin with twin baby boys and another with a newborn baby girl.

'Aww, look at the fingers and the nails, Amma. They are so tiny,' says my older daughter, instantly charmed.

There are two new babies at our school bus stop. Siblings of my daughters' younger bus friends. And now my daughters want a sibling of their own. A baby.

'I'm done!' I tell them. 'You've got each other. That's it.'

'But it will be nice to have a baby in the house, Amma,'

they say.

The husband agrees. 'Let's have one more. A girl. We've already nailed this whole "raising girls" thing. Kind of. Let's have another one.'

'I am certainly not putting myself through another pregnancy,' I state categorically.

'Then let's adopt,' says the husband.

'Yes, let's adopt a baby girl, Amma,' chime in the girls.

I give them an exasperated look. But to tell you the truth, I'm thinking about it. Just a little.

∫

I have always wanted to be a mum to a daughter. I even remember precisely when I decided this. I was a young adult, having just joined college, when I first saw an advertisement on TV for Santoor, a sandalwood soap. If you are my age, which shall remain unstated here, you know the one I am talking about. The one with a woman of indeterminate age, stylishly dressed in white pedal pushers and a pale yellow wrap around a crop top. This woman is working out in an aerobics class, when another girl in the class comes up to her and asks her *'Kaunse college mein ho?'* (Which college do you study in?)

'College? Me?' laughs the woman.

Just then a young girl, five or six years old, dressed in identical white pedal pushers and a pale yellow top runs up to her calling out 'Mummy' and hugs her. Cut to the other girl, who looks on stunned.

That's who I wanted to be—that woman hugging her daughter, the woman who looked young enough to be a college girl but was a mother. Did I rush out and buy the soap immediately? No. Even back then I knew enough not be taken in by an advertisement that promised eternal youth. But it was such a powerful image. One of a mother and her daughter. And their close bonding. I could imagine how it would be with the two of them. This image was imprinted in my mind. I wanted to be a mum to a daughter.

Many of my friends tell me that the advertisement made just as big an impression on them as well. Remember, this was a time when mothers looked like, well, mothers. They wore saris and if they ever stepped into an aerobics class, or wore pedal pushers, we certainly never heard about it. But here was a woman who was modern and cool, looked stylish and let's not forget, young. And yet, she was a mother. In hindsight, maybe I just wanted to be a yummy mummy, long before that phrase was even coined. A cool yummy mummy.

It's hard work, this business of being a yummy mummy. I have tried everything. Gymming. But I can't stand the sight of all those toned bodies. Jazz and salsa dancing. Of the Shiamak Davar variety. My knees, it galls me to admit, can't take it. Yoga. It's a no go. I am dizzy from all that breathing in and out. Belly dancing. Cool, right? The exotic music calls to me. But my hips? Oh, they DO lie.

I'm ready to give up. Almost.

The husband suggests long-distance running. I scoff. He probably has some vague vision of his golden years spent with a fit wife massaging his aching joints and muscles. Poor man,

I should leave him to his illusions.

'I run behind the kids all the time. That's as good as a workout,' I tell him instead.

'Yeah, and I am George Clooney,' he says.

I look at him. Right. He's got a point.

So I think about it. I hear the pulsating beat of the *'Eye Of The Tiger'* in my head as I imagine myself running. Tall. Slim. My face, fresh as a dewdrop, glowing with that radiant glow that every face cream and neighbourhood beauty parlour advertises and every thirty-something would kill for. A bouncy ponytail keeping step with my feet. I move gracefully. In slow motion. Like those *Baywatch* babes on the beach. With more clothes on, of course; maybe just a sliver of a taut midriff showing. But we do not live on the beachside. We live in the garden city Bengaluru. So I imagine running into the dreamy Milind Soman instead, on a gorgeous Sunday morning amidst the lush greenery of Cubbon Park. The poster boy for women's running in India is often to be found here on weekends. Or so the women runners in my city claim, flaunting their selfies with him on Facebook and WhatsApp groups.

The very next day I sign up to train with a running group.

Of course, I'm not tall. Or have a midriff. Or sport a ponytail. My short hair is usually plastered to my head. I run, desperately huffing and puffing to reach the finish line. And let's not even talk about things like perspiration. As for Milind Soman, in spite of my lurking around Cubbon Park almost every weekend, I don't even catch sight of him. Suffice it to say that our time has not yet come.

But I keep at it. After a fashion. It is a challenge though. If I have to make it for my Wednesday-morning workout with my running group, I have to plan like a grandmaster. School clothes, to be identified, ironed and set out the previous evening. Milk and breakfast items to be worked out in advance so the husband can get the kids started in the morning. I scramble through the run and rush back, cutting short the workout if need be, to comb their hair and make their ponytails just the way they like it. 'Appa can't make a ponytail to save his life,' state the kids tragically.

It's hard work, this business of being a yummy mummy. How come the advertisement never showed what went on behind the scenes? Not cool Santoor, not cool.

∫

I have always been a bit of an outsider, the odd one out, in the family I am married into. Remember, I am not your 'typical South Indian'. I had spent most of my growing years outside of South India. I looked, dressed and spoke differently. I had 'interesting' views on everything. Music? MTV Top-20 charts. The year we got married, Britney Spears released 'Oops! I Did It Again' and I could not get enough of that song or the boy bands that came after. I know, I know, I had (have) questionable taste in music. The poor husband, with his preference for classic hard rock and Ilayaraja hits was bewildered, to say the least. Clothes? Western, and especially sleeveless. I adore anything sleeveless. Makeup? Yes! Definitely no flowers or bindi. Jewellery? Minimal. Hair? Short. And left open and loose. In fact, the biggest concession I made to tradition on my wedding day was to agree to a braid. And then proceeded to go through the entire ceremony in a daze praying, 'Dear God, please don't let the false braid come off now.'

Quite a few nieces insist on calling me by name, while they call the husband 'uncle'. The kids are tickled pink at this. One of the nieces, who happens to be visiting us, tells my daughters, 'You know your mom used to be so cool. We all used to think she was the coolest aunt around.'

Used to be? Surely she means I *am* the coolest aunt around.

Sigh! I guess she is not too far off the mark. I can't believe they play Britney Spears in 'Retro Hour' on radio now.

Anyway, from being a cool aunt to becoming a cool mom was a no-brainer. Hosting three-day-long movie parties for the kids' girl gang to binge watch the *Harry Potter* series? Yep. Making MasterChef-inspired desserts? Yep. Bake-your-own-pizza-and-cookies birthday parties and taking the cookies home as return gifts? Genius, right? Letting the kids play in the rain? But, of course. Insisting that they eat their veggies and go to bed on time? Not cool, I know, but the answer to that is yes, as well.

'You know Amma, my friends said they had such a good time when they came over,' says my daughter. 'They said "Your mom is so cool,"' she adds in disbelief.

Mission accomplished, I thought.

It is a lot of fun having little girls around. My daughters have a few cousins, who are all, except for one, girls. I especially love hosting get-togethers and sleepovers for the girl gang. Other than providing them with food at regular intervals, one can pretty much leave them to their devices. They are old enough to entertain themselves. They turn on the music and dance. They play board games. Sometimes they venture into the kitchen to concoct weird drinks like lemonade with candy pops and sprinkles. They lounge about, exchanging gossip, chatting, giggling and generally have a good time. The highlight of the sleepover is the much anticipated 'midnight feast', *à la* Nigella Lawson. Just past midnight, they tiptoe into the kitchen, one behind the other in a line, from the oldest (and tallest) to the smallest. They rummage for snacks, which they then carry back into their room for a feast. It is all meant to be top secret. Of course I can hear them from my room, whispering and giggling. But one wouldn't want to spoil the fun now, right? That would be way too uncool.

The one thing that amazes me is that my daughters, who inevitably pick on each other when it is just the two of them, magically get along as soon as a third, either cousin or friend, joins in. Would it be the same if it was another sibling? I wonder. I can't believe I am actually considering this third kid business seriously. While I enjoyed their babyhood, I am also glad to have it behind me. I shudder when I think of the two-hour-long cycles of feed, burp, change, with nary a wink of sleep.

Will I have another kid? Maybe, I will. Maybe, I won't. After all, my dream of becoming a mum to a daughter has come true. Double-fold. Now if only someone would come up to me as I finish a run and ask '*Aap kaunse college mein ho?*'

> Ka mate, ka mate!
> Ka ora, ka ora!
> It is death, it is death!
> It is life, it is life!

14

Let's Do the 'Haka'

All has been quiet on the western front. West, as in England, where the English Premier League is being played. For some reason, my kids have been subdued. Perhaps the Liverpool Football Club has not been doing very well this season. I don't know. But I don't question my good fortune when the match viewing in my house comes down drastically.

Until, I walk in one Saturday evening to find my older daughter staring in rapt attention at the television.

'Shall we watch a movie?' I ask her. I know what the answer will be, but that doesn't stop me from trying.

'No Amma, there's a match on,' she says.

'Premier League?' I ask. 'Are we back to that? I thought you had gone off Liverpool, ha ha, what with them being on a losing streak and all,' I say, taking immense pleasure in needling her.

'Amma, that was football. This is rugby.'

'Rugby? Since when have you started watching rugby?' I ask.

'Just recently, Amma. The World Cup is on right now. It comes around only once in four years. The All Blacks are playing today,' she says. And then seeing the blank look on my face, she adds, 'The All Blacks are the New Zealand national rugby team.'

If I was the cursing sort, this would've been the moment for me to spew out some choice expletives. I had just been quietly celebrating the demise of football viewing in my house, only to be smacked right in the face with a whole new ball game. Rugby.

My daughter meanwhile has her eyes glued on the TV screen. She is watching what seems to be the highlights of a previous game, as they wait for the day's match to begin. It looks like a really aggressive game. There is tackling, grunting, pushing, shoving. Throwing each other violently onto the ground. The players of one team suddenly smack into the other team, interlocking tightly. They are packed closely together, their heads down, trapped in what seems to me a mortal combat. I am appalled.

'How can you watch such a violent game?'

'Calm down, Amma,' says my daughter, and then adds a tad superciliously, 'Yes, it might be a violent game, but there are rules governing it.'

'Are you saying that there are rules for beating each other to pulp? Murder even? And all is good as long as they follow these rules?' I splutter.

'Sure they beat each other up, but it's not gory or anything,' she says casually and then goes back to gawking at the TV screen.

'How can you let her watch such a violent game?' I ask the husband, pouncing on him as he walks into the room.

I glare at him. He gives me an innocent look.

I decide a new line of attack is called for. So I turn back to my daughter.

'What's the point in watching something mindlessly, a game that you know nothing about?' I challenge her.

'But I do, Amma. I know how the game is played. I know the positions, the rules, the teams.'

It seems she has been following the sport in the newspaper and what's more, the husband has given her a few links on the Internet so she can learn more. So much for that innocent look.

'See, there's the Loosehead Prop. And there's the Tighthead Prop. And here are the Blindside Flanker and Openside Flanker,' she says pointing to some players on the screen.

Knowing of her penchant for deadpanning sly comments with a straight face, I wonder if she is pulling a fast one on me. But no, these are actual player positions.

I get ready to walk out of the room in a huff, when I hear a sudden hush and what sounds like a war cry. I turn back to the TV screen. I see a group of players lined up in a triangle formation. Tough, rugged men. In tight black shorts. Suddenly, they have my complete attention.

The players stand tall, backs straight, with legs apart, and knees slightly bent. They look fierce and intimidating. Did I mention they were wearing tight black shorts? They begin chanting as they slap their thighs, stamp their feet and flex their arms. A war song. A challenge.

'That's the haka, Amma,' says my daughter. 'That's a traditional war dance of New Zealand's native Mori people. It's a tradition for the All Blacks to perform this before each game.'

Taringa whakarongo!	Listen carefully!
Kia rite!	Prepare yourself!
Kia mau!	Hold fast!
Ringa pakia!	Slap your hands against your thighs!
Waewae takahia kia kino nei hoki!	Stamp the feet as hard as you can!
Ka mate, ka mate!	It is death, it is death!
Ka ora, ka ora!	It is life, it is life!
Ka mate, ka mate!	It is death, it is death!
Ka ora, ka ora!	It is life, it is life!
Tēnei te tangata pūhuruhuru	This is the hairy man!
Nāna ne tiki mai whakawhiti te rā	Who caused the sun to shine again for me!
A Upane! Ka Upane!	A step upward! Another step upward!
A Upane! Ka Upane!	A step upward! Another step upward!
Whiti te rā!	The sun shines!
Hī!	Rise!

I can feel the goosebumps on my hands. The whole routine lasts less than a minute, but I am spellbound. I don't know if it's because of the menacing chant or the black shorts. I prefer to think it is the former.

'What's with the "hairy man"?' I ask my daughter, referring to a line in the chant. 'Hehe, none of the players look hairy to me.'

My daughter rolls her eyes and turns back to the TV, effectively dismissing me.

But I am curious. I wonder what the chants of the haka really mean. So I go searching on the Internet and come across the most captivating story. *Ka Mate*. That is the name of the song. It was composed by Te Rauparaha, the leader of the Ngati Toa tribe and it dates back to the early 1800s. The year was 1820 and it was wartime. Te Rauparaha was travelling across the lands to form alliances with other tribes. One day, the warriors of a rival tribe started pursuing him. Te Rauparaha was desperate to find a hiding place. That is when Te Wharerangi, the chief of a friendly tribe, came to his rescue. He hid Te Rauparaha in a food storage pit and then asked his wife to sit on top, so he would not be found. Soon the pursuers came to that tribe's lands. As they drew nearer, Te Rauparaha, hiding deep inside the pit could hear their footsteps. *'Ka mate, ka mate,'* 'It is death, it is death,' he cried softly to himself.

But by luck or, as some believe, due to some divine intervention, he was not discovered. One by one the pursuers finally began to leave. When Te Rauparaha heard their fading footsteps, he cried *'Ka ora, ka ora,'* 'It is life, it is life'. He then climbed out from the darkness of the pit into the light, to be greeted by Te Wharerangi (the hairy man).

And that is the true story behind the All Blacks haka and the hairy man.

Who knew that my kids' interests would result in my getting a cultural education of sorts? In any case, with all the stories I've picked up, I'm sure I'll be a hit at the parties.

Irate older daughter: Would you rather I feel comfortable or look good?
Me: Why can't you do both?

15

Sartorially Speaking

We are attending a wedding this weekend and I am going through my older daughter's rather limited wardrobe, looking for an outfit that will suit the occasion. All I see are faded track pants, shorts and T-shirts, and a few simple cotton salwar kameezes. As expected, there is nothing appropriate.

'Let me buy you a new outfit,' I tell her. She has long outgrown the few *pattu pavadais* and party dresses that she had, having hardly worn them at all. Her wardrobe could do with some new additions. Besides, I like the idea of shopping.

'Amma, I'm quite content to wear what I have,' she says quickly, wanting to get out of shopping for any fancy clothes. She has no patience for the clothes or the shopping.

'But none of these are appropriate wear for a formal

wedding,' I tell her.

'Why do I have to wear something formal or fancy? Why can't I wear something comfortable?' she asks.

'Why do you think fancy clothes are not comfortable?' I parry, rather weakly. I am not entirely convinced myself that such a utopian world exists.

This discussion about comfort versus style is an oft-repeated one between my older daughter and me, but I am quite surprised by what she says next.

'I am going to get married in track pants,' she says defiantly.

I don't know what surprises me more. Her sartorial choice or the fact that she has even considered marriage. Remember she is a pre-teen and currently, all things romantic are 'ewww!'

'Track pants? Pyjamas?'

'Yes. When I get married I will make that the dress code for my wedding. If other people can insist on formal or fancy wear, I can also insist that my guests come dressed as per my choice.'

That's my older daughter. Always looking for comfort when it comes to clothes.

Later, when I narrate this conversation to the husband, all he has to say is this: 'Think of how much we will save on her trousseau budget.'

I sigh. I wonder why I bother. The husband is the least bit interested in all things sartorial. I guess that's where my older one gets it from.

All this talk of weddings and pyjamas suddenly reminds me of an interesting titbit I had read a while ago.

'Did you know this bit of trivia about Nirvana?' I ask and the husband perks up at the mention of rock music. 'Did you know Kurt Cobain got married in his pyjamas, green ones, no less?'

'Really?'

'Yes. We should make sure the older one doesn't get to hear about stuff like that,' I tell him.

So, of course, he tells her. Immediately.

She is delighted. A rock star who got married in his pyjamas. What better validation could an almost-teen ask for?

'Apparently the bride wore a beautiful satin and lace dress, but he wore pyjamas. He said he was "too lazy to put on a tux,"' I tell her, hoping to curb her growing enthusiasm.

'Amma, it does not matter what you wear. What matters is who you choose to marry,' she says loftily.

'Whom you choose to marry,' I tell her.

'What?'

'Whom, not who.'

'Amma, that's not the point,' she protests, now irritated. It's fun to have fun, especially when it is at the expense of your kids.

'Well you know, that marriage ended in less than two years,' I tell her, changing tracks. I know it's a cheap shot and beneath me, especially considering how it all ended tragically because of his death. But one needs all the ammunition one can get when dealing with precocious pre-teens.

'Ok, Amma. I will remember that. Do not get married in green pyjamas. Any other colour will do,' she deadpans, her good humour restored.

Not wanting to spoil the good mood, I decide to shelve the shopping idea. Instead I go over to my wardrobe to see if I can find anything appropriate for her. She has just recently begun to fit into my clothes. Thankfully, we find a silk fuchsia pink kurta with a pair of cream coloured leggings that is elegant enough for my liking and comfortable and non-fussy enough for hers.

Having resolved one problem, I move on to my younger daughter. And I come up against yet another one. Only this time it is of the exact opposite nature. She has way too many options and is unable to decide what to wear. Indian ethnic or western formals? If the former, then a North Indian salwar kameez or South Indian *pattu pavadai*? Paired with matching bangles or bracelet? If western, then a flowery pouf dress or a white satin A-line one? Should she wear it with a shrug or go sleeveless? Will it be cold? Will there be mosquitoes? Choices, choices.

That's my younger daughter, the clothes horse. She can often be found standing in front of her bursting wardrobe mulling over the million dollar question: 'What shall I wear?' One might think it unfair that my two daughters' wardrobes are in such contrasting states. But my younger daughter likes clothes. She likes shopping for clothes. What's more, she has an older sister from whom she inherits hand-me-downs, especially the fancy ones, often in pristine state, sometimes even with the price tag still on them. For obvious reasons, these hand-me-downs do not include track pants.

My younger daughter has always enjoyed dressing up. *Pattu pavadais*, frilly party dresses, salwar kameezes, she adores them all. When she was younger, she had a white satin and tulle gown, with a delicate pin-tucked bodice and a wide purple sash, which was her absolute favourite. She wore it all the time. That it was not practical, for work or play, did not bother her. Comfortable? Not really, but it was great to twirl in and that is all that mattered.

We finally settle on a dress, the flowery pouf one, worn without the shrug, and paired with a bracelet. I can't wait to see what shopping for her wedding trousseau will be like.

⌇

Talking about shopping brings me to our biannual shopping expeditions. We usually shop once before the school year begins. This is the really easy one. Their school does not have any uniforms. The children are expected to wear simple, comfortable clothing: track pants with T-shirts and salwar kameezes. We usually walk into one store, pick up plain track pants and T-shirts in as many colours as the store stocks. We pop into the next store to buy fabric. Bold, bright colours for my older daughter and dainty floral patterns for my younger one. The local tailor takes care of making simple salwar kameezes with the fabric. That's it. We are all set for school.

And then there is Diwali. This is a more elaborate affair. We usually go shopping for new clothes a week or two before Diwali. My younger daughter and I, all excited. My older daughter and the husband, reluctantly and resignedly tagging along. The former armed with a book and the latter, his smartphone, to help pass the time. My older daughter wants to just get it over with. So she walks into the shop, looks desultorily at a few clothes, decisively picks one, tries it on and the deed is done. My younger one, on the other hand, is happy to traipse through many shops, trying on clothes, till she finds one, or two or three that she likes.

This year, for Diwali, my younger daughter wants a dress. Surprisingly, at the first shop we pop into, she spots something right away. A midnight-blue polka dotted dress. It is love at first sight. It is also very expensive.

So I hesitate. I don't ponder too much if the older one asks for an expensive dress. Firstly, this event is unlikely to happen since she is rarely interested in extravagant clothes. But on the off chance that she does pick an expensive one, I usually rationalize the purchase saying that the younger one can also wear it. Two for the price of one. But when the younger one asks for an expensive dress, it's harder to rationalize. Cousins who I could potentially hand it down to are all too young and I do not have the wardrobe space to store them till they are old enough to wear them.

'Where will you wear it?' I ask.

'Amma, I can wear it whenever we go out,' she says eagerly.

'Why don't we check out a few other shops? Look at some more options before we decide,' I say, trying to buy some time.

'But I like this one, Amma.'

'Are you sure you will wear it?'

'Yes!'

'It is an expensive dress and I don't want to waste money on something that you'll wear just once. You *must* wear it often,' I insist, before giving in to the inevitable.

'She's buying you the dress, but it comes with a free lecture!' quips my older daughter in an aside to her sister. They share a smile.

The joys of shopping with daughters.

As my younger one grows older, she seems to be getting more and more influenced by her sister. While she did buy that dress for Diwali, she does not dress up as often as she used to earlier. Increasingly, she seems to be showing a preference for track pants and T-shirts, like her sister. Now an evening out inevitably starts in tears. One or both of my kids end up angry or upset. And it's all thanks to me and my disapproval of their decision to wear faded, worn-out track pants to a fine dining restaurant. My friends tell me that the situation will change soon enough. That in no time at all the kids will be teenagers and they will want to wear mini shorts and halter-neck tops. Then I will be the one in tears, angry and upset.

∽

The one common thing that seems to interest both my daughters now is, surprisingly, my clothes. They constantly eye my clothes, my accessories, my footwear. They immediately notice if I wear something new or different. They are also ready with expert comments on how it looks on me.

Say I wear something unusual, and ask my younger daughter for an opinion.

'How do I look?'

'Amma, you look nice. But I don't think this dress is quite your style.' Ouch.

The most common refrain though is, 'Can I wear this when I am older?'

My older daughter can't wear my shoes. 'I have inherited Appa's big feet,' she says ruefully. But she makes free with my clothes. Now that she fits into my clothes easily, she looks forward to borrowing my clothes for special occasions.

On a holiday in London last summer I picked up a leopard print top. Those who know me will realize this is a bold design choice for me. I am prone to picking more sober, elegant clothes.

'Sober? Elegant? Hah, that's just another word for B-O-R-I-N-G,' said the husband. 'I dare you to pick the leopard print.'

When it comes to sartorial choices, he is of course clueless. But he was having so much fun at my expense that I decided to call his bluff. I bought the top. And to my surprise, I loved it. The chiffon fabric felt light and soft against my skin. Who would've thought that I was the sort who could carry off a leopard print?

A week later, my older daughter needed a top for an event. As expected, her wardrobe yielded nothing. We opened mine and the leopard print top caught her eye.

'Can I wear that?' she asked.

'Sure,' I said.

She tried it on.

'Can I keep it?' she asked excitedly, which was rather unusual for her, considering we were talking about clothes.

'Sure,' I said and that was the end of my very brief love affair with leopard prints.

All this borrowing and sharing has left my younger one quite worried.

'If she takes everything, what will be left for me, Amma?' she asks.

'You can have all of my stuff when I outgrow them,' says the older one.

'But I want Amma's clothes!' says my younger one stubbornly.

She mulls over it for a while and decides on a new, proactive course of action. Ask first, think later.

'Grandma gave me a new pair of earrings. It's very pretty,' I tell her one evening on our way back from my parents' home. My older daughter is away at a friend's house.

'Show me, Amma,' she says eagerly.

'I'll show you when we get home.'

'Ok. But Amma, you must save it for me and give it to me when I am old enough to wear it,' she says.

'But you haven't even seen it. How do you know if you will like it?' I ask her.

'That's ok. You have good taste. If you like it, it must be good.' She is obviously eager to stake her claim before her sister can see it or ask for it.

'You know you could buy all the clothes, shoes and accessories that you want when you are older. You don't have to wait for mine,' I tell her.

'But it's not the same as wearing yours. I want to inherit yours,' she says.

Although I pretend to moan and groan when they ask for my stuff, I must admit I am secretly thrilled. I find my eyes lingering on them when I catch a glimpse of them wearing my clothes and accessories. The younger one, tottering in my heels. The older one, turning her head this way and that to feel my favourite long dangling earrings swish. Sometimes I catch sight of them preening in front of the mirror, when they think no one is watching. A secret smile on their faces. Squaring their shoulders, a sense of pride at finally becoming big enough to fit into their mother's things.

I am determined to enjoy this while it lasts. Especially since it means that I now have a good excuse to expand my wardrobe a little. After all, I do have to share with both my daughters.

It's time to go shopping.

Older daughter: Amma, please tell your younger daughter to come to the bus on time in the evening. I can't keep watching out for her till the last minute.
Younger daughter: But I am on time. The bus starts at 3.40 p.m. and today I was there exactly at 3.40 p.m.

16

Hold the Bus

This morning I went in to wake up my daughters as usual. Same time, same words, same tone.

'Girls...time to wake up *kanna*'

'My head is hurting, Amma,' said my younger daughter.

'Is that so? Where is it hurting?' I asked.

'I said head, Amma.'

'But where on your head?'

'All over my head,' she paused and added, 'My stomach too.'

'Which part of your stomach?'

'All over, Amma.'

'Why don't you come and drink your milk and then see

how you feel?'

'I don't want milk.'

'Then what about school?'

Silence.

I was quite surprised. Both my daughters enjoy going to school and almost never ask to take a day off. Maybe she was feeling under the weather. But then, my younger daughter is also prone to a bit of drama. Maybe she just wanted some attention. Whatever the reason, I was unsure and decided to leave her alone for the time being.

While my older daughter set about getting ready, the younger one lounged in bed. A full twenty minutes later, she suddenly sprang out of bed and came hurriedly to drink her milk.

'What happened?' I asked.

'I'm getting ready for school.'

'But what about your headache?

'It's gone now.'

'And your stomach ache?'

'That's gone too.'

'Are you sure?'

'Yes, Amma. Now I have to get ready. I can't miss the bus. There's a birthday picnic in school today.'

Whatever was her original reason for wanting to skip school, it was obviously not serious enough to warrant skipping cake and a fun birthday picnic.

And so I sent an SOS message. To a WhatsApp group that the parents at our bus stop use to communicate with each other—bus delays, route changes, kids running late and so on. My fingers trembling, I typed in, 'Hold the bus.'

Hold the bus. Every parent has surely sent this message at one time or the other.

At my daughters' bus stop, over the years, we have been privy to a lot of high speed, James Bond style chases. A boy wearing one shoe running to catch the bus. His mother running behind him, with his other shoe in one hand and a sandwich in the other. A mother in a car, screeching to a halt right in front of the bus, just in time for her kids to scramble out of the car and into the bus. Yet another father racing behind the school bus. His little hatchback bravely chasing the big yellow bus all the way to the next stop. A mother run-walking to the bus stop to make sure the bus doesn't leave without her son (this was in the pre-WhatsApp era). The son strolling in languidly, as teenagers are wont to do, with his iPod earphones glued to his ears.

In all this, the children seem to be cool. It is only the parents who are stressed.

What is with kids and tardiness?

This is one vexing problem that seems to afflict all kids sooner or later. Even kids who start out being punctual in the early years, seem to fall prey to this once the teenage years roll by. We often exchange notes, the parents at our bus stop, looking for tips on how to get the kids to be on time.

Set the alarm ten minutes early, or even set the clock back by ten minutes, suggests one. Waking up seems to be the biggest problem and most of my friends complain that getting their kids out of bed in the mornings is the hardest part. They resort to everything from coaxing to pleading to hollering, and as in one case, even threatening to sing. I must confess, I do not have this particular problem, today being the rare exception. My daughters are early risers. Always have been. Unlike the husband and I. We struggle to get up most mornings and often wonder where they have inherited this gene from.

In my house, waking up my daughters is the easy part. But getting them out of the house on time is a different story altogether.

'Run the morning strictly like a drill sergeant,' advises a friend.

'No, let them be,' argues another.

'If we let them "be", they will never get on the bus.'

'That may be so. But the kids will learn only if they make mistakes. Let them learn to manage their own time responsibly.'

We briefly debate letting them miss the bus if they are late and spend the day at home. Alas, the consequences are not appealing in the least. Who wants a bored kid or, as in my case, two bored and squabbling kids, on their hands?

Morning routines are filled with strife. A friend tells me, every morning her kids fight over who gets to use the bathroom first. This, in spite of their house having multiple bathrooms. That sounds like a familiar tale to me.

But more than bickering with each other, especially as they approach the teen years, a general lethargy seems to have taken over my daughters. Increasingly, there seems to be a tendency to dawdle.

They have taken to lingering over their toilette.

I catch my younger daughter making big soap bubbles with her hands, when she is supposed to be brushing her teeth. When questioned, she has a ready answer: 'But Amma, it was you who asked us to wash our hands well.'

I prod my older daughter, asking her what's taking so long, and nudge her to get going. She too has an answer: 'But Amma, it was you who asked me take out the tangles in my hair. Didn't you say it looks like a bird's nest?'

How did their tardiness become my fault?

Breakfast is no quick affair either. More often than not, they are engrossed in the book propped up in front of them. If I take the book away, they stare instead at their food, lost in a daydream. It does not help that the husband choses just this moment to kick-start the morning by playing the latest Tamil film song on his phone.

Hey excuse me Mr. Kandaswamy...

'Oh no,' groans my older daughter. 'Oh yes,' exclaims my younger daughter, delighted to sing along. The song is a mad caper. It has a pair of jousting lovers, the two of them calling each other everything from *uppu muttaye* (sack of salt) and *ducku muttaye* (duck's egg), to Kashmir and Pakistan, and Hitler's granddaughter and Lincoln's grandson. What's not to love?

Breakfast, of course, is forgotten.

A pal tells me, her kids have no time for breakfast because they have just spent the last twenty minutes in their rooms, in front of the mirror. The son playing air guitar to Nirvana and the daughter with her hairbrush in her hands, crooning Taylor Swift's latest post-breakup love song. The joys of teenage kids.

And then, of course, there is the last minute rush. Amma, I'm supposed to carry a shoebox to school. Can you give me one? Can you cover my notebook? Make my ponytail? Help me tighten my shoelaces? They rush out the door, only to come rushing back since they have forgotten their art kit or their water bottle or their jacket.

I often lose my cool.

'It's unbelievable how we always end up in a tearing hurry every morning. This, in spite of waking up so early,' I complain.

'All that's fine, Amma,' they say, rolling their eyes. Of course, they have to have the last word. 'Have we ever missed our bus till now?' they smirk.

I guess this is one battle I am not likely to win.

'Arsenic may have gained notoriety as a deadly poison, but it is useful in many more ways than just to bump off your nearest relative so that you can inherit a huge fortune!'
—Entry from my middle schooler's Chemistry project

17

We Don't Need No Education

My older daughter has got arsenic on her mind. Her class has been studying the elements in Chemistry and they have each been asked to pick an element to research for a project.

'I picked arsenic, Amma' she says.

'Arsenic?' I ask, surprised by her choice.

'Yes. My first choice was gold, followed by silver. But they were both taken. So I picked arsenic.'

'You do know that arsenic is a poison?'

'Why do you think I picked it, Amma?' she asks with a wicked glint in her eye.

Ostensibly, it is a Chemistry project on elements, and she is supposed to do her research on arsenic's properties and form and so on. But what has really caught her attention is your garden variety death by arsenic poisoning. Take the case of Napoleon Bonaparte. There are many conspiracy theories surrounding his death. Was arsenic the culprit? Was he deliberately poisoned? Or was it unintentional, a result of prolonged exposure to the toxic fumes from the wallpaper in his home? In those days arsenic-based pigments were commonly used in making green dyes for wallpapers. The jury is still sitting on that apparently.

Then there's the queen of murder, Agatha Christie. My daughter is quite thrilled to discover that arsenic was Agatha Christie's poison of choice. Over eighty victims were poisoned across her books, and the most common poison used was arsenic, probably because it was such an easy chemical for people to acquire at the time.

Curiously, there is also the case of the people of San Pedro de Atacama in Chile. They have been drinking water that is contaminated with arsenic all their lives, and it is believed that they may have developed some immunity to it. There's more, several cases about arsenic poisoning from around the world—accidental and deliberate, fictional and real cases. Chemistry, it seems, has suddenly become very interesting, eclipsing even Mathematics for the time being.

Her favourite tale though is a real story that happened in 1858. A nasty tale of humbugs, adulteration, accidental switching and very real poisoning. Here's what happened. William Hardaker, aka 'Humbug Billy' was a sweet seller in Bradford, England. He usually purchased his humbugs or boiled sweets from Joseph Neal, a sweet maker. Now Neal used to often substitute sugar with 'daff', since sugar itself was very expensive. One day, Neal sent his lodger to a pharmacy to buy supplies, in particular, daff. The pharmacist's assistant, who was standing in for his sick boss, however, mistakenly sold arsenic trioxide instead of daff.

Neither the lodger nor Neal realized this. Neal made and sold a whole batch of humbugs to Hardaker, who in turn sold it to the customers in his shop. This batch ended up poisoning over two hundred people. Tragically, twenty-one people died. The story ends with one positive outcome though. As a result of this incident, The Pharmacy Act 1968 was passed in the United Kingdom leading to the regulation of adulteration of foodstuff.

Nothing excites my daughter more than facts and the tales behind the facts.

'All this interest in arsenic poisoning is quite morbid, you know,' I chide my daughter. 'Should I be worried?'

'Amma, can I get you some sugar for your tea?' she deadpans.

∽

So far school has been fun for my daughters. A little too much fun, if you ask me. But then I grew up in a different era. I grew up to the anthem of Pink Floyd's 'We Don't Need No Education.' When I look back, all I remember is the stress of my own school years—the homework, the projects, the exams. My daughters, on the other hand, seem to enjoy going to school. Whoever heard about kids looking forward to school?

My daughters rarely get homework from school. But when they do, it is quite unconventional.

One evening, my younger daughter came home all excited.

'I have a big project, Amma. You won't believe it Amma, it

will take me a whole month to complete it.' Picture my daughter, eyes wide, voice animated and hands gesticulating wildly. My younger one has always been prone to a bit of drama.

'One month?' I ask.

Turns out they were studying the moon at school. Their assignment was to go out and look at the moon every night. They then had to draw what they saw in a small booklet, charting the moon's shape and position in the sky. One page for every night. At the end of this process, you could flip the little booklet and see the moon in motion.

So every evening, for a month, I accompanied her to catch sight of the moon. It was fascinating to see the progress as the month went along. Soon enough, we had a full flip book. I can't tell you who was more excited, my daughter or I. Now compare this to what I remember of my homework. Learn the times tables up to 16×16. Are you sure you learnt it? Say it another twenty times till you are sure. Complete four pages of handwriting practice in English and Hindi. And much worse.

Now take the case of my older daughter who is in middle school. All they seem to do are experiments and projects. She is forever asking me, 'What will happen if I do this?'

'What will happen to the yolk if we shake the egg before we crack it open? Will it be all squished up inside?' We tried that at home. In case you were wondering, the answer to that is no. Egg yolks have a thin membrane covering them and also a set of ropes called chalazae which anchor the yolk to the centre of the egg. So a simple shake is not likely to impact it much. But go ahead, try it out for yourself. Just be prepared to have a few slip through your fingers though.

There's more.

'What will happen if I heat salt?'

'If we melt this 530 ml slab of frozen ice cream, will it still fit into the same half-kg box?'

'How long will it take for this lemonade to freeze?'

'What do you think will happen if we dip the thermometer in the boiling rasam?'

The thermometer will go bust, in case you were interested. I have one at home as proof. The home thermometers used to read body temperatures are not built to rise to the boiling point of water, 100 degrees celsius. Since the reading is off the charts, the thermometer goes bust.

Is it any wonder that my daughters like school? The good news is that since my daughters are not stressed, I am not stressed either. No rushing out at the last minute to buy geographical maps or pictures of freedom fighters or chart papers or any such thing. The great news though is that I'm the envy of all my friends. Their evenings and weekends are often spent 'helping' their kids with assorted projects and homework. They tell me they'd like to let the kids do it on their own, but are worried about how their child's work will fare when compared with others who've had 'help'.

And then there is the dreaded four letter word. Exam.

Come exam time, everyone vanishes. Parents. Kids. If you do manage to bump into anyone, say in the lift, the air is fraught with tension. The parents have their heads down. As do the kids.

'Hey, what's up?' I say.

'Exams,' say the parents.

'Oh...' I say sympathetically.

'No television. No playtime. No phone calls. No friends or visitors to the house,' add the kids morosely.

'When do your exams start?' they ask us.

'Ninth,' my daughter replies.

'Oh ninth of December. You don't have much time, do you? How is your preparation coming along?'

'No aunty, ninth grade,' says my daughter. 'In our school, exams start only from the ninth grade.'

'Oh!'

Jaws drop. Silence ensues.

I look down. I'm afraid my secret glee will be visible for all to see.

All this lack of stress in our day-to-day lives has set me thinking though. Are the kids too chilled out? Are they having too much fun and not being serious enough about academics? This especially comes home to me in light of a recent incident. We had just had a nice and relaxed weekend. The kids had lazed around, caught up on the previous week's episodes of *MasterChef Australia*, read a fair bit, and generally chilled out. Come Monday morning, just as she was getting ready to leave for school, my younger daughter remembered that she had some pending homework. She had gone on a school trip to the zoo the previous week, and the teacher had asked them to either draw or write about what they saw at the zoo. She had forgotten all about it, until that very moment.

She quickly pulled out a sheet of paper from a drawer. First, she drew a vague shape, a lump for a body. Then four lines sticking out from the bottom of the lump, the legs. Two dots for eyes, two ears and a curve for the mouth.

'What is that?' I asked.

'It's a lion,' she said as she folded the paper, ready to put it into her bag.

'Is that it? Are you sure you are done?' I wanted to say more, so much more. But I restrained myself, given the fact that she had to leave right away in order to catch the bus.

'Oh wait,' she said. She whipped out her pencil and masterfully drew a swish of a line for the tail.

Voila, now she was done. One hundred and ten seconds to complete the weekend homework. I was dumbfounded. Should I marvel at her unfazed manner and confidence in having averted a near disaster or cry at her easy comfort with turning in such a careless job. As for the picture, I found it hard to identify the lion in that lump. And I was her mother, a very biased one at that too.

Come evening, I rolled up my sleeves, ready to deliver the much-needed lecture. I asked her if she turned in her homework.

'Yes, Amma. You know what aunty said?'

'What?'

'She said, "You write such wonderful poems, why don't you write a poem to go along with this picture you made of the lion you saw at the zoo?" So I am going to write a poem right after I finish this snack.'

She then proceeded to do exactly that. A creative poem with a well-thought-out structure and form. Even I couldn't fault.

A bullet dodged this time.

This incident has made me rethink my approach. I decided I am going to get a little more involved with their studies. Monitor the two of them more closely. So I question them every day.

What did you do at school today?

Did you have Science class?
English?
How did your 'End of Module Review' in Hindi go?
What did you do in Math?
Do you have any homework?
When is it due?

I hover.

Do you think you should research a little more on the Constitution of India before you attempt answering the questions?

Why don't you practise saying the poem out loud a few more times?

Let's revise the boy and girl words in Hindi again and then let me quiz you.

I think the story ends too abruptly. Why don't you flesh it out a bit more?

Why don't you write down the sums more neatly on a fresh piece of paper?

Don't be so casual about your work. Why don't you take an interest in it?

'Isn't it enough that I do my homework, Amma? Why do I have to "take an interest" in it?' asks my older daughter.

Sigh.

> 'What Amma says is usually good for you. What Appa
> says is not good for you, but it is always fun.'

18

What's in a Word?

'When can we pack?'

This is the question the kids have been asking me since morning. It's that time of the year, mid-term break and school will be out for a while. They are going on a holiday with their cousins in a few days and they can't wait. They have been on trips before without us, excursions from school. But this is the first time they are going away with cousins and they are excited.

The younger one is mildly anxious about being unable to sleep at night. Of late, she has been prone to nightmares. So I give her a small stuffed squeaky hamster to hold on to. I tell her, if she feels anxious she should squeeze it and the squeaky sound it makes will remind her of me. And that, in turn, will remind her of me reprimanding her for some transgression. Obviously no nightmare can be worse than that image. I am joking, of course. Trying to make her laugh and forget her fears.

She looks at the stuffed toy and gives a slight smile.

'Yes Amma, it will remind me of you since it looks so different from you and your austereness,' she says.

I am taken aback.

'Austere? Do you know what austere means?' I ask.

'Yes. It means strict, stern,' she says casually.

You could've knocked me over with a feather. I can't quite get my head around this. Both, the fact that she knows the word austere and that she thinks I am austere.

I sidle up to my older one and ask her, 'So your sister thinks that I am austere. Ha ha. What do you think?'

'Yes, you are,' she says, without even looking up from the book she is reading.

'Austere? Really?'

I am shocked, completely blindsided.

'Yes, you are stern…' she begins, but as she casually glances up, she sees my obviously crestfallen face and hastily adds, '…ish. Sternish.'

Well, I never.

'All parents are a little stern,' I tell her.

'No, there are many people who are not austere,' she says.

'Then who according to you is not austere?'

'Appa.'

I am cut to the quick.

∽

Later that night, I lie in bed, unable to sleep. I feel the walls crumbling around me. It upsets me that the kids think of me as austere. When did I become the bad cop?

Obviously, someone in the family has to lay down the rules. Some limits, reasonable limits. That would be me. Some of those rules are non-negotiable. Like going to bed by nine on school nights or saying no to junk food or keeping the house clean. Someone has to enforce those rules. Guess who? Me again. There are exceptions to the rules, of course, and guess who decides? Me, of course.

But I always thought I was a fairly liberal parent. A cool mom. Letting them break a few rules here and there. Encouraging them to pursue what interests them, involving them in decisions related to them. No pressure, no expectations except that they put in their best effort into whatever they do. And yet, that is obviously not how they see me.

I definitely do not like the image that the word 'austere' brings up. Am I too severe? Harsh? Rigid? Controlling?

Seeing me toss and turn, the husband asks me what the matter is. Reluctantly. This is me. He is aware he will get nothing short of the long version of the story. It is late and he would rather sleep.

I narrate the whole conversation with the kids and ask him what he thinks. 'Am I austere?'

'Well, you are stern…ish,' he jokes, copping out by quoting my older daughter. He can always be trusted to see the funny in everything. But I am not amused.

Mulling it over, I wonder if the kids meant to use the word austere. They probably do not know the severity and the starkness that a word like austere conveys. They were of course complaining about all the rules they have to adhere to, like most kids are wont to do. But as a parent I know kids need limits as much as they need their freedom. I know I am particular about and insist on some things. But I also know I am not unreasonable. I *know* I am not too strict. No, it cannot be that.

So, what is it? What did they mean?

How is Appa not austere, but I am? What does he do that I do not? I am determined to get to the bottom of this.

Over the next few days, I watch them. The husband and the kids.

While I am busy watching them, the kids have also been watching me, it seems. We have been lazing in front of the television. When an advertisement comes up, I catch my older daughter giving me an appraising look.

'What is it?' I ask her.

'You and Appa are not very affectionate with each other,' she states disapprovingly.

'That's not true,' I retort.

'See that advertisement? You are not like that couple.'

The advertisement shows a couple, a young Caucasian one, saying goodbye at the airport, arms around each other. Violins in the background. Deep longing looks. Fingers grazing. Romance is in the air.

'But what does romance have to do with what they are selling? What are they selling? Do you remember?'

She doesn't. But that's besides the point. The husband and I, with no deep longing gazes, no overt public displays of affection, did not measure up to my daughters' expectations.

When we were younger, we were subjected to disapproving lectures on the impropriety of public displays of affection, PDA as it is called now, from our parents. Now that we are older, we are being subjected to disapproving lectures from our children on the lack of PDAs. Next, they'll want violins playing in the background.

We live in India, what do you expect, I want to tell my daughter. But I catch myself. Is there some truth in what she is saying? Am I not openly affectionate? For a moment let's forget about the husband. What about the kids? Do they feel the lack of hugs and kisses? Am I not affectionate enough with them? Is that what they mean by austere? Am I too severe in manner?

I squirm slightly. Growing up, we were not a family that hugged or used words of endearment casually. We were not the touchy-feely sorts. Maybe it was a different generation. Or maybe it was just my family. So yes, I am a little uncomfortable with expressing affection physically or verbally. It was easier to cuddle and coo sweet endearments when the kids were babies. Maybe I have not been as free with my hugs and kisses as they have grown older.

Unlike the husband, who is always ready to pull them into a bear hug, tickle them silly, cuddle them and cootchie-coo them. 'Appa...' they protest. It embarrasses them sometimes, and that is precisely why he does it, I suspect. But underneath all that embarrassment, they are probably delighted by the indulgence.

Is that why Appa is not austere and I am? Or is it something else?

Admittedly, he is more fun. He is always game for a tickling match. Or any game, for that matter. Cards, Pictionary, Monopoly, Sudoku, Crossword, football, badminton. You name it, he is ready to play. And inevitably, he is a riot. This reminds me of another conversation we had some time back.

'Amma, you don't do anything with me,' complained my

younger daughter one day.

'Who made that special gulab jamun dessert for you? And who made sure your bicycle seat and brakes got repaired?' I asked.

'Amma, I am not talking about what you do for me.'

'Then?'

'I would rather you do something with me than something for me.'

Oh.

Have I become so caught up in getting things done, that I no longer do things with them? Am I guilty as charged?

Am I not fun anymore? Was I ever fun?

One of the enduring memories that I have of my daughters' childhood is that of this one rainy day. We even have a video of this day titled 'Rainy jump'. We are visiting my parents. I am with my then two-year-old elder daughter. She is running around on the lawn when suddenly, it begins to drizzle. My parents call out to us to come back in, out of the rain. The drizzle turns into a shower. The husband picks up an umbrella and comes out to give us cover and help us back in. But my daughter will have none of it. She is so thrilled to see the rain coming down. She calls out to her father to come and play. But he promises to watch her, safely from under the umbrella. She calls out to her grandparents. But they are busy recording this video from the balcony. She calls out to me. I look at her, exuberant, elated, her eyes alight with excitement, and know I will cherish this moment forever. She takes hold of my hand and starts running. She runs round and round in circles, jumping in the puddles, splashing me, taking me with her. We stick out our tongues to catch the raindrops, and giggle when it lands in our eyes instead. When did I go from being the mom who cavorted in the rain with her daughter to being called austere?

Maybe it *is* time to lighten up a bit. To cut myself some slack. The housework and chores will probably not get done. In fact, I am *sure* they will not get done. But the kids are growing up so fast. I decide some fun is what the doctor ordered. So the next evening I challenge my younger daughter to a game of Uno.

'I hope you know that, I am the master of the Uno-verse.'

She rolls her eyes at my lame attempts at punning.

There is nothing the little one loves more than a good game. She is high-spirited and a good sport. In the end, I trounce her.

'You might as well give up. Today is my day,' I crow with delight, completely caught up in the excitement of winning.

But she is not the least bit flustered.

'Amma, maybe today is your day. But remember, some other day will be MY day.'

Touché.

Later in the week, they are all set to leave on their trip. I have a million instructions for them when my older daughter interrupts me with a smile.

'Amma, can I give you a hug? I like hugging you and squeezing the breath out of you.'

'Yes, and you squeak just like my hamster,' laughs my younger one, joining in the group hug.

Austere? What's in a word?

Third Term:
January–March

From: MyKids@Bengaluru.com
To: Amma@gmail.com
Date: Friday, 19 February 2016 at 10.12 AM

Subject: Third Term—Open House and Parent-Teacher Interactions March 2016

Dear Parent,

Greetings!

As we near the end of the academic year 2015–16, it is time to meet the teachers who have interacted with your child. We will be holding an Open House on 11 March 2016 where you can see a display of all the work that the children have done in the course of the last two terms. You will soon be receiving your child's annual report and subsequently, the parent-teacher interactions will be held between 14 and 18 March 2016.

We look forward to meeting you.

Kindly note that the last working day for the school children will be Friday, 31 March 2016. As always, we would like to insist that the children attend school till the last working day.

With warm regards,
Principal

> 'Tik tik tik tik tik...'
> 'Amma, your friend is calling.'
> —My cheeky younger daughter on hearing the lizard chirp in our kitchen.

19

There's a Lizard in My Kitchen

I don't know what I would do without the husband. No, I am not ashamed to admit it. Mind you, I am not your average Jane, damsel in distress. But he is certainly my knight in shining armour. Who else can I depend on to shoo away the dangerous intruders in our home—lizards? That and file my income tax returns.

Yes, there is a lizard in my kitchen. I don't quite remember when it wandered in and took residence in the kitchen loft. It just announced its presence one night with a loud staccato *tik tik tik tik tik*.

'I think there is a lizard in the house,' I tell the husband as I lie in bed.

'Hmmm,' he says, half-asleep.

'Can you hear that sound? That's the typical chirping of a lizard. You've got to drive it out.'

But he is already asleep.

For days I wait, apprehensively, but I don't actually see the lizard. I keep hearing it though. At all times of the day and night. *Tik tik tik tik tik...* And then it happens. Early one morning, I walk into the kitchen and I see it perched on the wall. I do what any self-respecting person would do. I squeal. Loudly.

'What happened? Why are you screaming?' asks the husband and kids who come running, having been woken up so dramatically from their sleep.

'I saw that lizard. You know, the one that has been making all the noise these last few days? You've got to drive it out.'

'Was it big?' asks my younger one, rubbing her eyes sleepily.

'No, I think it was of medium size.'

'Then why did you scream?'

'Excuse me, I did not scream. I squealed. There is a difference, you know.'

The husband grabs a newspaper and rolls it up. That's his weapon of choice to shoo out the lizard. My hero. He opens all the kitchen cupboards and bangs on the loft doors loudly to get the lizard to come out. But there's no sign of it.

'You know Amma, some time back, when you were out, we found another lizard in the kitchen,' says the younger one, now fully awake after all the ruckus that the husband has created.

'What? When?'

'The service person for the water purifier came one day when we were at home with Appa. When he took the machine off the wall, a lizard ran out from behind it.'

'Seriously?'

'Yes. It was big and it looked so gross and yuck,' she says with a lot of drama, especially when she sees me squirm.

'Do you remember that other time when a little lizard wandered into the living room from the balcony by mistake?' asks the older one, now warming up to the subject.

'Yeah and Amma jumped onto the sofa and started screaming,' says the little younger one, hamming it up. She is quite delighted at the opportunity to make the most of what was most assuredly a minor incident.

'You had not yet come home from office that day, Appa,' she adds.

'It was just a baby lizard. How can you be scared of a baby lizard that is just the size of your little finger, Amma?' asks the older one, quite amused.

I glare at the two of them. They smile back.

'Who says I am scared? I am just not as generous as you girls are about sharing my abode with other creatures,' I say, making a subtle dig at their never-ending travails with head lice.

'Ha!' snorts the younger one.

'I think it ran out, back to the balcony, when it heard Amma scream. Poor thing, it must've been terrified,' says the older one. 'You should've seen it, Appa. It was so funny,' she chuckles.

This is getting out of hand.

So I ask, 'Shouldn't you girls be getting ready for school?' This douses their good mood, quite effectively, and they move on.

As for the lizard, there's no further sign of it that day.

But the incident happens again the next morning and the day after. The lizard makes its appearance, like *Suprabhātam* every morning, to wake me up from my sleepy daze. I squeal again. Alas, this time no one comes running. I stomp into the bedroom and give the husband an ultimatum.

'Either the lizard stays or I do.'

He turns over and continues snoring.

So I do what all damsels in distress with snoring knights in shining armour do. Take matters into my own hands. I device a new 'entry into the kitchen' routine. I stand well outside the kitchen and first turn on the torch on my phone. Next, I lean all the way into the kitchen, shine the light from my phone onto the light switches and then quickly turn them all on at one go. I lean back and count to five, take a deep breath and then step into the kitchen. It's fast, this lizard-in-residence. I must give it that. It is usually gone by the time I walk in. Occasionally I catch sight of its wriggling body as it vanishes into the loft, its tail swishing behind it. It is enough to give me the shivers.

'This means good news, Amma,' says my house help when she hears the *tik tik tik* sound that morning. She tells me that a lizard chirping is considered holy and auspicious. I don't take her seriously until, of course, Google verifies it. Apparently if you are talking with someone and you hear a lizard chirping, then whatever you were saying will come true. If only I knew how to get the husband into a discussion about that much-longed-for foreign holiday at the exact same time that the lizard chooses to chirp.

There's more. Google, as usual, is a treasure trove of information. Did you know that a lizard falling on you has a special symbolism? Depending on the day of the week, time of the day, which direction it falls from (north, south, east, west), and where it falls on your body, it could mean different things. On your hand, leg, back, stomach...the options are endless... your hair, head, nose, upper lip, lower lip... Although I am hard-pressed to understand how you could possibly make out the difference between a lizard landing on your hair and head, let alone upper lip and lower lip. I would be too busy screaming my lungs out. But that's just me.

Just thinking of the permutations and combinations of day, time, direction and position is mind-boggling. Then again, Math was never my thing. The bottom line though, is that each one foretells different things. Good health, bad health, financial gain, financial loss, new friends, new spats, it can predict future happenings, even your mental stability. As for the last one, I could've told you that myself. I don't need some pseudo psychic to tell me that I'm freaking out, going insane, with a lizard in the house.

The next morning, my house help walks into the house and announces, 'It is not good news, Amma.' She has just come from another house that she works in. The lady of that house has told her categorically that lizards are very inauspicious and dangerous. 'That madam says to keep a peacock feather. That will drive away the lizard. Or else eggshells, Amma. That will work too.'

I don't put much store by all these superstitious beliefs, but I certainly wouldn't mind seeing the last of the lizard in my kitchen. I'm not quite sure where I will get the peacock feathers though. I have seen people selling all sorts of things at traffic signals, from plastic bobbing plants for car dashboards to rainbow-coloured umbrellas to feather dusters. Maybe I should keep an eye out. In the meanwhile, eggshells it is.

Every day, I carefully save the shells after serving the kids eggs for breakfast. Then I place them at strategic locations. My kitchen is now lined with eggshells, little domes of white, balanced precariously on the window sill, above the cupboards, on the edges of the shelves, on the kitchen slab, and of course, in the loft.

It has been a week. A week of me treading on eggshells. A week of no lizard sighting or hearing. It's early days yet, but I am cautiously confident that I may have solved the lizard problem.

So I let myself relax. Let my guard down, just a little bit. I contemplate throwing away all the eggshells. I even walk into the kitchen bleary-eyed, no more of those early morning kitchen entry manoeuvres for me. When suddenly, out of nowhere, I hear it. *Tchak tchak tchak tchak tchak....*

༄

'Why so glum?' asks the husband when he sees me sitting slumped on the sofa that morning.

'There's a lizard in the kitchen.'

'Oh? I thought you said it was gone. Didn't the eggshells do the trick?'

'Yes it did. This is a different one.'

'How do you know? Have you seen it?'

'No. This one is different. It sounds more masculine.'

'Seriously?' he asks incredulously. 'You can make that out from its call?'

'Yes,' I insist stubbornly.

'So how does this one sound? Does it have a deep baritone voice? As against the earlier shrill female one?' he asks, his lips twitching.

'Laugh all you want. But I know this is a different one.'

'Girls, there is a new male lizard in the kitchen. Check out his deep baritone voice,' he calls out to our daughters.

'I'll need more shells,' I say distractedly, as I see them all leave the room suddenly in a rush. I hear what sounds suspiciously like chortles from the other room. They can't have been laughing at me, can they? No, I must be mistaken.

Later that evening, I walk into the kitchen and there I see it, sitting there, its head raised, calm as can be. The lizard. A big, fat, gross-looking one. Definitely a different lizard. The husband has followed me into the kitchen. I turn around and give him a triumphant look. Ha, see? Nothing gives me more pleasure than saying, 'I told you so!'

The husband springs into action. A broom in one hand, a rolled up newspaper in another. It's a cat and mouse game. Only there is no cat and no mouse either. Just the husband and the lizard. It seems like a long time, but in what must've been no longer than a couple of minutes, he manages to chase it out the balcony door.

I look at him. My hero. I forget that I had spent the whole of last weekend in a huff, angry at him for some imagined and real slights. All is forgiven. Sigh, after this episode I will be indebted to him for life. Or at least this week.

Her: Amma, your mission, should you choose to accept it, is to come to our school this evening and pick us up *after* sports day.

Me: But what about my Sunday afternoon nap?

Her: This message will self-destruct in *five, four, three…*

20

Mission Accomplished

I have always found it strange and hard to accept that given a choice between watching a movie and watching a football match, my daughters would pick the match. Every single time. With the possible exception of the *Harry Potter* movie series. It's not that they don't enjoy a good story. They are voracious readers and have relished different genres over the years. But not so with movies. They have always shied away from watching movies. Perhaps the sensory overload was too much for them. The combined impact of the visual and sound effects can be a little overwhelming, scary even, for some children. Don't ask me how they sit through the *Harry Potter* movies though. J.K.

Rowling and Harry Potter are no mere mortals, after all.

I did not realize how unusual this disinterest in movies was until I heard friends, other parents, often talking about weekend movie outings with their kids. I was torn. Another friend, a film-maker by profession, was shocked when she heard that my daughters rarely watched movies or TV. Hearing her, a professional in the industry, wax-eloquent about some classic movies and what insights and experiences they had to offer, decided it. Utterly convinced now that my children's education was sadly lacking, I decided to take matters into my hands. Some reel-life education was called for. I decided I would introduce my daughters to the silver screen, one movie at a time.

So, what should we begin with?

'Animation films?'

After all they are made with the express purpose of entertaining kids.

'Nah. Too kiddish,' my daughters shrug.

'Comic capers?' Surely that would be right up their alley.

'Meh.'

'Classics?'

'Too long.'

'Romance?' I joke.

'Eww!'

'Sports movies?'

'Hmm, maybe. But we'd rather watch that Liverpool match first.'

I was almost ready to give up in frustration. When suddenly, the darnedest thing happened.

'Amma, you know, my friend was telling me about this movie that she saw recently,' said my daughter one day.

'Oh?'

'It's called *Mission Impossible*. It seems there's this guy called Tom Cruise and he is a spy. And he is always given the most impossible of missions. It seems this new one that my friend saw is the fifth movie in the series.'

'Oh?'

'I believe he does all these really awesome stunts.'

'Oh?'

'Apparently, he is quite good-looking.'

'Oh...'

'Amma, I'm not saying he is handsome. My friend said so.'

'Ok.'

'So, do you think you could get us the older movies in the series? And do you think we could maybe watch the latest movie in the theatre?'

And just like that, we found ourselves ensconced in the plush PVR IMAX cinema, gasping as Tom Cruise did the impossible—hung on for dear life from the side of an airborne plane.

Which leads me to believe that sometimes it is better to drop all elaborate schemes, and just let the adolescent weakness for handsome Hollywood heroes and peer influence take its due course. All in all, mission accomplished, I say!

'Amma, YOU are the tooth fairy!'
—*Insists my younger daughter, even as I attempt to evade the matter with artful prevarications.*

21

The Tooth Fairy Has Left the Building

Ever heard of the tooth fairy? I hadn't either until my daughters came along. I first stumbled across her in a children's book of American origin. In case you are among the lucky few who have not heard of the tooth fairy, according to folklore when children lose their baby tooth, if they keep it under their pillow, it is believed that the tooth fairy will swoop into their room in the dark of the night, take the fallen tooth and leave a small payment behind.

I came across the tooth fairy roughly around the same time I was working my way through the books *I Want My Potty!* and *I Want A Sister!* with my older daughter. If I seemed a little manic in my enthusiasm for these books, all I have to say in my defence is that my older daughter was three years old and in addition, we had a newborn baby in the house. Between potty training and sibling rivalry, I needed all the help I could get. Anyway, that was about the time I came across another book in the *Little Princess* series called *I Want My Tooth*. My older daughter was fascinated by the idea of a tooth fairy who could exchange her fallen tooth for a present. She couldn't wait for her tooth to fall out. The younger one, of course, was a long way from getting a tooth, let alone losing one.

And so we waited, my older daughter and I, with bated breath, for the first tooth to fall out. It took a long time coming. In the meanwhile, my younger daughter managed to sprout teeth, learned to bite and soon joined her older sister in the vigil, waiting for that first tooth to fall and the tooth fairy to visit.

When the big moment finally arrived, my older daughter was so excited. She couldn't stop showing off her 'gap'. All day long, she and her sister spoke about the impending visit from the tooth fairy. I knew I had no choice. I would have to magically conjure up a tooth fairy. But no coins for this one, I decided. The tooth fairy would get a thoughtful present, something that my daughter loved most. A book. That night I helped my daughter put her tooth under the pillow. When she woke up next morning, she was so happy that the tooth fairy had lived up to her expectations and more.

And so it began. Having set down this path, I had no choice but to keep to the course. When my younger daughter lost her first tooth a few years later, it was by accident, not natural causes. She had been perched precariously on a dining chair when it suddenly tilted. She fell and her tooth went flying out.

Her first question once we had ascertained that she was not hurt in any other way was this: 'Amma, will the tooth fairy still come, even though my tooth did not fall by itself, but broke because of an accident?'

As the years went by, the tooth fairy kept adding to my daughters' book collection, adeptly pocketing their teeth. From time to time, the kids would wonder who the tooth fairy was and how she knew that it was time to visit. But it was an idle question. They were still young enough to believe.

And then one day, my older daughter lost another tooth just as she was brushing before going to bed at night. Usually, I have a little notice before a tooth comes out. First, they complain about a shaky tooth. Then, they take to fiddling with it, pushing it in all awkward directions, especially when I am around since they know that I find this disgusting and gross. I know then that it's time for the next present. But this time I had no notice whatsoever. I did not have a secret stash from which I could pull out a book and it was too late to go to the stores. So I began rummaging around, looking for some ideas. That's when I came across a miniature perfume bottle that someone had gifted me. The bottle was a collectible and it looked so pretty that I hadn't had the heart to use it. With no other options in hand, I quickly wrapped it up. Next morning, my daughter was astonished and delighted. She loved her books. But with this very grown-up gift, a whole new world seemed to beckon. The younger one looked on enviously. Needless to say, I had to go out and buy another miniature perfume bottle for the tooth fairy's next visit to her.

This incident had unexpected ramifications. Firstly, it upped the ante. Just books alone were no longer enough. Surely the tooth fairy would come up with more exotic presents the next time around. Secondly, they started to get more suspicious about who the tooth fairy was. They took to questioning me at length, trying to wheedle out the truth.

'Amma, you put the present under my pillow, didn't you?'

'No, I did not.'

'But I saw you tiptoeing into the room.'

'Yes, I came into your room to check on you.'

'Amma, you are the tooth fairy!'

'I did not put anything under your pillow.'

You will note, that not once in the course of our conversation did I claim not to be the tooth fairy. I only insisted that I did not put any present under their pillows. And I kept insisting the same thing over and over again. I had after all taken the precaution of delegating the job to the husband. It was he who retrieved the tooth and placed the tooth fairy's present under the pillow. The kids never dreamed of suspecting or interrogating him. Semantics, one might say. But it enabled me to prevaricate, without having to lie outright.

The kids, of course, tried every trick in the book to get me to confess that I was the tooth fairy. My younger one was especially relentless, and wily too. We would be in the middle of some activity and she would suddenly, out of the blue, ask me: 'Amma what do you do with all the teeth you collect from under our pillows?'

'What teeth?' I would say, just about managing to keep my wits about me.

With time, I knew that they knew. And they knew that I knew that they knew. But still, we carried on playing the game. The husband, however, had had enough. After one too many last minute trips to the store to pick something up, he put his foot down. By now the older one had braces on and it did seem like it was time. The tooth fairy had had her run and we agreed that it was time to bid farewell. We decided to do so in style. We printed out a letter from the tooth fairy to the kids and left it one night under each of their pillows.

Dear kiddo,

Hope you have been good and brushing your teeth regularly.
As you probably know, my job involves a lot of flying about and tiptoeing all through the night. I can tell you, it has been very tiring!
So I have decided to RETIRE. That's right, RE-TIRE. This is my last day at work and I won't be coming around again.
Don't feel too bad—if you miss me, you only need to brace yourself!
Bye,

The Tooth Fairy

My older daughter wasn't overly bothered by the farewell. By now she was old enough to be amused by such shenanigans. But my younger one was unwilling to give up so easily. The next time a tooth fell, she insisted on keeping it under her pillow. When no present turned up, she laughed good-naturedly and redoubled her efforts.

'Amma, I'm going to try again. See? This is where I'm keeping the tooth,' she said saucily. 'Just so you know. Not that you are the tooth fairy. But I'm just telling you.' Such cheek. And she kept at it, night after night. The husband was quite immune to her charms. Not me. A week later I caved in. The next morning, she woke up to find the tooth gone and a candy bar under the pillow.

After this episode, she took to following the same tactic every time she lost a tooth. She would make a big fuss about putting her tooth under the pillow and following it up with a cheeky 'Amma, you might as well give me a present!' I resigned myself to the inevitable.

And so it was, until yesterday.

The apartment complex we live in has been actively working towards sustainable living, with waste segregation at home being a key focus area. We now separate our organic waste that will be composted, from the dry waste that will be recycled, and other reject waste that will be sent to a landfill. The children have also been instructed on this and they keep coming to me with questions on what should be disposed where.

Yesterday, while I was busy making dinner, my younger daughter came up to me and asked me, quite matter-of-factly, 'Amma, my tooth fell today. With the new way of garbage segregation, which basket should I throw my tooth in—the organic waste, dry waste, or the other reject waste?'

Sigh, it's the end of an era. Looks like the tooth fairy has definitely left the building this time.

Me: You are so like your father.
Her: I know who I am most like. I am most like myself.

22

Milestone Mammas

Is she? Is she not? Is she? Is she not?
That has been the hottest topic for debate in my family. She insists that she is. I insist she is not. The husband decides to settle the matter once and for all. He lines us up against the wall, mother and daughter. He pulls out a measuring tape. Going by the wild cheers that follow, one would think India had beaten Pakistan in the Cricket World Cup finals. But no, it is only the most anticipated event in recent history.

I believe she is. Taller. By a quarter of an inch.

As my older daughter shoots past my shoulders, it is another big milestone in our lives. Now I'll have to master the art of glaring down at my daughter while looking up at her.

All roads lead to Rome. In case of milestones, they literally do. Milestones were originally stone pillars that were used in the Roman Empire to mark distances on the roads. In fact, Emperor Caesar Augustus famously had a monument erected in the centre of Rome. Called the Miliarium Aureum or the golden milestone, all roads were said to begin from here and all distances were measured in relation to this point. Which is probably how the phrase 'all roads lead to Rome' came to be.

History lesson aside, milestones are the most important mantra of the modern parent. And they begin even before the baby comes along.

Married a year? 'Do we hear the pitter-patter of little feet?' Nudge nudge, wink wink. Time to get to work. Pregnant? Finally. Nausea? Did you feel the baby move? Did it hiccup?

Delivered? Congratulations! Is the baby sleeping through the night? Can he hold his head up? Is she turning over? Can he sit? Crawl? Pull herself up? Walk? Talk? What about school admissions?

Crossing a milestone. That heady rush. That sense of achievement at ticking one more item off the list. Secretly thrilled that you are ahead of the curve.

As a new mom, I was eager and enthusiastic. I read books and scoured the Internet all the time. As soon as I found out I was pregnant, I bought books by the dozen. I signed up for weekly updates from, not one, but two leading websites. I wanted to cover all my bases. I put in my due date, and voila, like clockwork I would get weekly emails telling me what my foetus was up to that week.

Week 10: Your foetus has now developed finger nails and toe nails.

Imagine that! I did wonder though. How would I verify that my foetus had in fact, actually reached this milestone? Well, the short answer to that is, I couldn't.

I was quite the intense mom, especially the first time round. Watch for progress, not deadlines, my paediatrician and all the parenting books and websites told me. So of course, I watched for deadlines. I tracked everything. Height, weight, gross motor skills, fine motor skills, language skills, cognitive skills, social skills.

Month 9: Did she crawl? No. But that's alright. She had bypassed that and moved on to pulling herself up and started walking, all by eleven months.

Year 2: Could she talk? Well, does using conjunctions like 'because' in complex sentences by month twenty count?

(Drum roll! I had a genius on my hands.)

In the early months I even kept a diary. To track how many hours my baby slept, when, what and how much she ate. And no, I did not keep track of how often she pooped. At least not in the diary. What do you take me for?

And then, along came my second daughter. With the older one starting kindergarten, a busier husband, me starting a new job, more mess, more work and less help around the house, it was all just too much. Too much to keep track of the little details, even for a supermom like me. I was busy and tired. But surprisingly, I was also calm and confident. Maybe I was an old hand at this. Or, maybe the novelty had worn off. I realized that it wasn't that big a deal. A month or two, this way or that, wouldn't make a big difference in the long run. Imagine my daughter filling out her college application. What were the chances that she would see this question in the form?

Question 13: When did you master the 'pincer grasp'?

The only milestone I kept track of was the scheduled visits to the paediatrician. He would do a complete check-up, tell me all was fine and I was happy with that.

The husband now tells me that our younger daughter has flourished under my benign neglect.

∽

As a baby, my older daughter used to suck her thumb. Having read contradictory reports on the matter, I went to the paediatrician armed with a questionnaire.

'It's her birthright to suck her thumb,' he said grandly.

He used to say that a lot: 'It's her birthright to reject food if she is not hungry'. 'It's her birthright to wake up five times at night' and so on. I knew with experience that it was pointless to argue with him when the child's birth right was involved. 'How long is it okay for her to suck her thumb?' I asked instead.

'Say, till she is around four years old.'

So come fourth birthday, I had a game plan. The first thing I did was to rope in my daughter on the project. We were on a mission to disengage the thumb from the mouth. We fashioned gloves from a shiny pair of stockings to put on at night, so that she wouldn't be able to put her thumb in her mouth. We put up a chart prominently in her room to display the gold stars she would get for every night that she managed to not suck her thumb. Right on track, within a few weeks, the thumb sucking stopped. Mission accomplished.

Same story with my second daughter? Err, not really. Her fourth birthday came and went. I kept telling myself that I would start the disengagement process soon. Weeks turned to months. I rationalized thinking, 'I don't know anyone who has sucked their thumb into their teens or adulthood'. So I did nothing. Sometime after her fifth birthday, the habit quietly vanished. I don't exactly know when or how. But it happened. Uneventfully.

∽

While I am quite the 'involved' parent when it comes to such things, I like to think that I am reasonably non-competitive. But all it takes is one birthday party, one play date, one visit to the park, to make me think again. Everywhere I turn, I trip over milestones and mommies waiting to share their triumphs. It is enough to make even Zen-mamma turn into hen-mamma.

'My son already knows his A, B, C's and numbers up to 10…say it for aunty, *beta.*'

'My daughter is fully potty-trained… Oh you haven't yet trained yours? But school is just six months away. What will you do?'

Did I brag too? After all, I had an Einstein, Beethoven and Leonardo da Vinci all rolled into one (nay, two) on my hands. Yes, of course, I bragged. Sadly, only to my mother. Who else would be interested in listening to me go on and on about her favourite, and at that time, only grandchildren. On the positive side, there is nothing quite like mutual admiration for a baby to bring a mother and daughter closer.

As the years go by, and my children hurtle into their pre-teens and teens, it is becoming harder and harder to remember all the milestones. And there are so many. What remain with me are only the moments, the flashes of memories, the odd patchwork of emotions. Besides, who ever said milestones had to be set in stone? Does it really matter if one's first tooth comes in at nine months instead of six? Isn't it enough to know that it did and that there will be no more gummy grins to tug at one's heartstrings?

A niece sends me a video on WhatsApp of her son turning over. 'So cute,' I admire. 'He turned over on the fourteenth of last month,' she says. I laugh and tell her, ten years from now she will not remember much of this. She confidently tells me that she has bought a baby album and she is recording every milestone in the book. I want to tell her it doesn't matter. To forget the book and just enjoy the moment. That the milestones are only as good as the memories.

Years from now, I might not remember exactly when my daughter shot past me in height. But I will remember that walk back home from the basement car park one balmy spring evening. Feeling the transience of time. Feeling it keenly. A strange sense of loss. A yearning for what once was. And also anticipation for what was to come. But most of all, what I will remember is the look of sheer delight on my daughter's face as she casually swung her arm over my shoulders. Just because she could.

> Me: Lost in your thoughts?
> Her: No Amma, just sifting through mine.
> Just because somebody is not communicating, it doesn't
> mean that they are lost in their thoughts.
> I'm perfectly anchored in my thoughts.

23

Is This the End?

'Amma, are you coming to the school for the Open House?' asks my older daughter as yet another school year draws to an end.

'Yes, I am.'

'How are you planning to come?'

'I'll come with you in the school bus.'

'Oh.' There is a pregnant pause and then she says, 'But you can't sit next to me, ok? My friend will sit there.'

From insisting on sitting on my lap to now saving a place for her bestie, we've come a long way indeed. In case you are wondering, no, I am not upset. Not at all. So what if my not-so-little girl does not want to sit next to me? Why should I be upset?

I narrate this little incident to a few friends, parents whom I meet at school that day.

'Kids grow up so fast,' they commiserate. 'Poor you! You must have felt so hurt.'

Am I? My daughter is growing up. And that is as it should be. So what if she does not need me all that much anymore? This is what I have been waiting for a long time, isn't it? Freedom.

I spent a fair part of my daughters' early years waiting for them to grow up. So I could get away. There have been times when the sheer monotony, the daily grind, the constant clinging and neediness, the sleep deprivation, they have all got to me. But this is not a job you quit or walk away from.

So I waited. Waited for them to grow up so I could finally put my career back on track, travel more, get on top of my reading list, catch up on movies, pursue that hobby, socialize more. I waited for them to grow up, so I could go back to living my life.

Now that it looks like I might get my wish after all, why should I be upset?

When I was younger, I used to love wearing crisply starched cottons, especially the *Lucknawi Chikankari* salwar suits. I was single, carefree and had all the time in the world to spend on my wardrobe. Once the kids came along, they had to be relegated to the back of my wardrobe. The cotton suits, not my kids. I no longer had the luxury of time on weekends to wash, starch, dry and iron them. Grubby hands pulling at my kurta, wrinkling it up by climbing into my arms or nestling on my lap. It was all too much. I switched to the more practical wash-and-wear *kurtis*. My leggings became my new best friends. They had come into fashion then. I had a rainbow of colours in my wardrobe. They covered a multitude of sins and even managed to make my legs look longer and slimmer.

Now maybe, after all this time, I can finally pull out my beloved *Chikankaris*. So why the does the prospect not fill me with excitement and anticipation?

∽

In the early years, while both my daughters were attached to me, my younger one was especially clingy. My little *chipko*, I called her. She probably came into the world, took one look at her older sister and knew instantly that she would have to fight for my attention. So she latched on to me and hasn't let go ever since.

Back at the Open House at school, this year they have planned a short performance by the children. This is a culmination of all that they have learnt in performing arts during the academic year. I keep my eyes focused on my younger daughter, ready to wave to her as soon as she spots me. I know she will search for me in the audience, her eyes seeking reassurance. But she is in the midst of her excited group. The children, aged between eight and ten, are all animatedly whispering amongst themselves on the side of the stage. They wait for their cue, walk decorously on to the stage, take their positions and get off to a rousing start.

The energy is electric, their enthusiasm infectious. My daughter catches my eye midway through the performance and grins. No reassurance needed there.

The audience erupts in applause. The kids take a bow. Then my daughter skips away with her friends, chattering and giggling. She does not look back. I feel proud and yet, strangely bereft.

∽

'How did you ever manage to send me to the hostel, away from home?' I ask my mother. I have memories of her sending me off quite cheerfully. Every single time that I came home for holidays and such. Even at my wedding. Having been brought up on a staple diet of Bollywood movies, I had imagined my *bidaai*, or send off, in glorious technicolour. I had imagined a scene straight out of a Karan Johar movie. Joyful tears, in true filmi style.

My parents' unfortunately hadn't read the same script. Nary a tear was shed. After the wedding ceremony, my mother and father, came to drop us at my new home. A quick cup of coffee, and then they said bye and left. That's it. Yes, I had been living alone on my own in a different city for many years by then, first at college and then for work. So it was not like I was leaving home for the first time. And yet. Their only daughter was getting married and all I got from my parents was a casual 'Ok, bye'. I didn't know if I should be offended.

'Surely a bit of crying is warranted at weddings and farewells,' I remember saying indignantly to my mother, many years later.

'I am heartless that way,' she jokes.

'I'm never letting the kids go,' I say, only half-jokingly. 'I'm quite sure I can even find them grooms in the apartment complex that we live in. There are one thousand two hundred apartments here, surely there must be a few "suitable boys".'

My mother smiles at this and says, 'The joy of parenting is in seeing you live your life. Our pleasure is in knowing that we have raised you to stand on your own feet, and be independent. Your father and I are of course here to support you, should you ever need our help. But this is your life, and you have to live it. By yourself.'

Will I ever be that wise when it comes to my daughters?

I hope so. I hope I can help you find your wings. I hope that when the time comes, I can let you fly away. But I am not letting go without a few tears. A copious amount of tears. Grace and dignity be damned!

Acknowledgements

To Anita Nair, thank you for your advice, guidance and mentorship. This book was just a dream till I came to Anita's Attic. You helped me find my voice and gave me the confidence to boldly chase my dream. I will always cherish your warmth and generosity.

I'm grateful to Sudeshna Shome Ghosh, for believing in this book and for always making the time to dispel my constant doubts. To Elina Majumdar and the team at Rupa – thank you for your commitment to this book. Gerard Britto, thanks for all the design gyan.

To my friends, thank you for the many kind words of encouragement and support, especially the promises you made to buy my book. I'm going to hold you to it.

I'm thankful to my mother for being my biggest champion. For all that you have done and been, I'm grateful to you. Thank you, to my father for being the pillar of strength, and my brother, for always being in my corner.

Thank you, to my husband, for being the man that you are. For putting up with my many moods and still deciding to stick with me. And for the endless cups of tea. No one does it like you.

And finally, my daughters. When I was younger, if someone had told me that such a large part of my identity would be tied to that of being a mother, I would've scoffed. But then you came along and you changed everything. Smart, cheeky, kind, silly, sweet, pesky - you girls are my everything. Thank you for all the laughs. What a ride it has been.